TALES FROM MOGADOR - KASHA AND THE KIFF

Kasha Kermould

Dawson

To all those who have touched my heart, and whose hearts have been touched by mine.

FOREWORD

This is a piece of fiction and is entirely the work of the author. Unless otherwise indicated, all the names, characters, businesses, places, events and incidents in this book are either the product of the author's imagination or used in a fictitious manner. Any resemblance to actual persons, living or dead, or actual events is purely coincidental.

CONTENTS

Title Page
Dedication
Foreword
One Dirham   1
She Of The Many Smiles   4
A Stick In The Eye   7
The Belly Dancer   11
The Jbala Network   15
Geckos   18
The Coach   22
Hanging Trainers   26
Flaky Skin   31
Khamsa   35
Financials   40
Sousa   44
Aziz   48
A Phial Of Potion   52
Hilal   56
An Uneasy Alliance   60
Pink Lipstick   64

Hussain	69
Aid	73
A Bottle of Whiskey	76
Tangier	80
The Radar Station	84
The Truth	86
Ankles	92
Help Me!	97
Red Flags	101
A Tray Of Cakes	106
The Phone	110
The Macadam	114
Questions, Questions…..	118
Checkpoint	123
The Well	127
Scoring	133
A Pdf	140
Trust In Allah	144
Damaged Stock	148
All At Sea	152
Ingrid	156
All Is Not Lost	161
Souad	166
Once Bitten	170
Acknowledgements	175
About The Author	177
	179

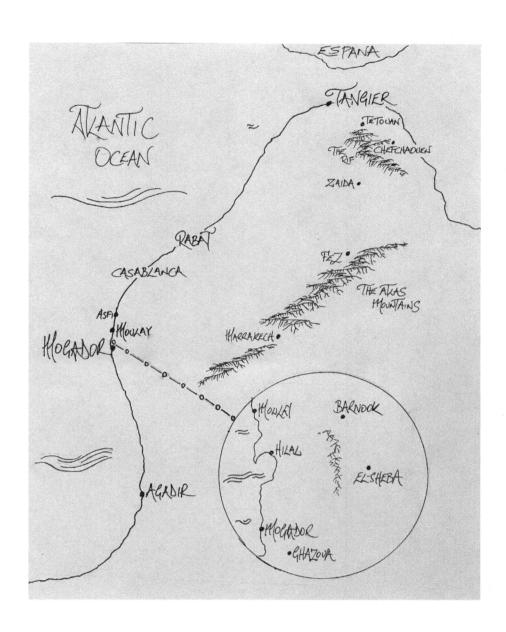

ONE DIRHAM

I'd been sceptical about the plan when I first heard it. I'd even laughed out loud when Otto had finished talking me through the idea. He'd caught the bus into Mogador from Ghazoua, where he was living with his Moroccan boyfriend, to drink coffee and proposition me with the hair-brained idea he and Ingrid had been cooking up. She lived round the corner from him, and they'd been strategising ever since Marek's desperate plea had appeared in Ingrid's inbox. So I'd laughed, and almost fallen off my chair, when Otto stopped explaining and stared at me. The level of jeopardy associated with the sketchy undertaking was huge. It was almost certainly going to end in prison sentences, the loss of a lot of money and quite possibly injury or even tragedy. Why on earth would I ever agree to become part of such a scheme? Otto looked at me, with his old grey-blue German eyes, his mouth slightly open revealing his false teeth, and said, 'Well what do you think?'

'I think you've finally lost any sense of reality my friend,' I replied.

Sipping my black, stomach turning coffee. I turned my gaze from Otto, and watched the traffic flow pass the King's palace that was almost immediately in front of the cafe where we sat. The authorities in this country would not be sympathetic nor merciful should they become privy to the plan Otto and Ingrid were germinating. There would be a heavy price to pay for disobeying the laws of the state and monarch in this country. The Moroccans know this, and I should have taken heed as I watched the colourful and noisy scene in the road before me. Otto lit a cigarette, and waited for my reaction. Sometimes people don't do the right thing though, and I was about to make one of those decisions. I'd listened to Otto, been entertained by the ludicrous stupidity of his proposal and yet had turned back to him and said,

'Okay, I'm in.'

*****

Driving home to Moulay, against the sirocco wind that hustles dust and probably misadventure from the north of Africa, my motorbike rumbled underneath me with a slight unease. To the west lay the Atlantic Ocean, and to the east the rural landscape was dry and arid. Should I have seen the dead and decomposing donkeys on the roadside as omens? Perhaps. My meeting with Otto though had set me on course for a potentially thrilling and life changing experience. One that I had accepted, against all reasonable consideration, and whose consequence I was now going to need to accept. Had I known what would befall me, and the intense fear I'd have to become accustomed to living with, I'm certain I wouldn't have made the decision I did. There was no going back now though. Otto had my commitment, and already I'd organised a 'business' rendezvous with both Mustaffa and Ayoub. They'd be keen on the money, but less so on the risk.

While I was mulling over the hazards and fearful scenarios that the pair would no doubt bring up as reasons why they should get a higher percentage for their nefarious contacts, my eye was caught by a sparkle on the road just up ahead. For a moment I wondered whether I'd really seen anything at all, but then there it was again, something definitely sparkled just beyond my front tyre and then disappeared under the bike. Parking beside a rough and windswept stone wall, I followed the broken edge of the road back towards the glimmering object that I'd driven by. Crouching down to get a better look, I squinted in the bright sunshine, only to find myself looking directly at the King's head. For there by my feet was a one dirham coin, dropped or lost, and found by me, on the road home to Moulay.

SHE OF THE MANY SMILES

It was late afternoon by the time I arrived at Bab Doukkala, the northern entrance gate of Mogador's fortified medina. The arched stone gateway, designed in the 1750's by French architects and built from the local 'manjour' sandstone, is only a few minutes walk along old, rutted cobbles to the mellah district. It can nevertheless take you longer as the streets are narrow and winding, and packed with a milling blend of Moroccan Arabs, Amazighs, Africans and a spattering of europeans. The mellah, or Jewish quarter, was infamous for its salt which among other things was used by the town's authorities to persevere the severed heads of criminals that they displayed as a warning at Bab Doukkala. This practice has been discontinued but the mellah, with its proximity to the ramparts that overlook the ocean and the dark, damp, mouldy stains that cover its walls, made for an eerie welcome to the medina.

I was there to meet Alison, a prized and important contact of mine that fate had brought across my path shortly after arriving in this North African country. Known by her farmer husband as, 'she of the many smiles' her local knowledge and uncanny wisdom had become indispensable to me. So, in an echo of King Saul's visit to seek guidance from a medium at Endor, I had arranged to sit and share tea with Alison, in the hope that she'd shed some sagacity on the decisions before me. From the mellah I wound my way past the fish market. It is a dirty place, especially under foot where blood and guts mingle with posses of cats tearing at fish heads.

Further on, the sickly sweet smell of dead chickens and

boiling goat's feet lingers in the air, giving this part of the medina a scent of medieval drama. I've learnt that it's best to avoid eye contact with the shopkeepers, who are never short of curiosity and opportunism, and who'll spot the blue eyes of a stranger from farther away than you or I can see.

Alison's house was deep within the labyrinth of interconnecting and shady passageways that provide seclusion and security in the heart of this fortress sea port. The walls of these passages rise four floors to the blue sky, and are adorned with arabesque and Islamic decor, some of which is crumbling from disrepair.

I knocked on the thick wooden door to Alison's home, waited a moment and then heard a small window above me open. 'Come on up, Kasha,' I heard her say as I caught a flash of her welcoming smile and her grey hair disappearing back inside.

The door handle was an owl's head, cast in metal, and warm to touch. The spiral staircase up to her living room and kitchen was dark, save for the small vertical slits cut into the wall, like daggers of light. She was sitting at a table in the dim room, incense burning and a tall candle lit in front of her.

I pulled up a chair. She smiled again, a considered and inquisitive one this time, and tilted her head as if she was asking me a question. We exchanged greetings in Arabic; she'd become influential, along with Ayoub, in my learning the language. Although, unlike Ayoub, she had insights into the mystique of the language and had cultivated some expertise in Sihr (magic). So it was that through our Arabic interchange she quickly sensed an uncertainty in me. She poured us both a cup of hot black tea, and we sat looking at each other, with the flickering light of the candle between us. After a little while she turned her gaze from me as though in a trance, and said, 'The weather is not good for fishing, it will change in a short while, but will still be dangerous and deadly.

I bit my bottom lip. This was really quite an odd and

incongruous remark to make, however it sounded like the advice, or at least the insight, that I had hoped she might reveal. I hadn't mentioned anything to do with fishing or for that matter my meeting with Otto, but somehow, in my stomach, I knew she was making a reference to the scheme Otto had talked me into. In the biblical story of Saul his medium conjures up a message of doom, which he chooses to ignore and suffers terrible consequences. I wanted to believe, trust and act on Alison's foretelling. If I understood her cryptic message correctly she was proposing caution and patience.

We finished our tea over a discussion about our respective vegetable gardens, and began to say our farewells.

'All sorts of plans cross our path Kasha,' Alison said smiling, as I stood by the top of her stairs. 'Those that kindle your desire, and for which you set aside your fear, are the ones that will fill your living days with treasure.'

I paused, studied the age lines around her eyes, and raised my own eyebrow in reply. As I made my way out through the medina, and the maze of the evening jostle, I couldn't help suspect that every wrong-doer who'd had their head cut off, and stuck on a pole over the gate at Bab Doukkala, had been following their desire and seeking treasure.

A STICK IN THE EYE

Time can pass slowly in Morocco, and without any apparent consequence. Arrangements, on the other hand, can change very quickly. So it was that I'd thought better of meeting both Mustafa and Ayoub together. It made more sense to talk through Otto's scheme with Ayoub first, before unravelling the whole plot to Mustaffa. I left a voice message for Ayoub, a common occurrence in a land of illiteracy but got through to Mustaffa and stalled him with an excuse about the urgent need for me to clear the well in my garden. Ayoub called back shortly after, and we agreed to meet in a small village called Ain Lahjar, equidistant from our respective homes in Mogador and Moulay. The village, at the heart of a very fertile and sheltered inland valley, is blessed with a plentiful supply of water that is pumped all day from the limestone seam through which it seeps. To reach Ain Lahjar both Ayoub and I would need to ride our motorbikes, from different directions, across the arid forested coastal plain, over the ridge of sandstone hills that look down upon the Atlantic, and into the cultivated land beyond. By the time I reached the narrow stony track that leads into the village I could see that Ayoub had already arrived, and his bike was parked on its stand by the mosque.

It was Friday, I parked up too, and then sat on a sunny doorstep within eyesight of the mosque as a trickle of djellaba-clad men made their way past me and into the mosque. I mused that perhaps these older bearded men might be a touch late for the jumma, but time being as it is in Morocco, this was probably irrelevant. A group of little boys, too young to do salat, gathered on the corner near me, unaccustomed to the presence of a european but perhaps reassured by the keffiyeh round my neck and my calm, almost uninterested demeanour. After a while their curiosity in me waned, and except for one chap who continued to pull wheelies and ride his makeshift mountain bike back and forward in front of me, every one left. I could just overhear the prayers from the mosque, and waited in the dusty warmth of the sunshine for my Arab friend to complete his devotion. One of the many complicated aspects of Ayoub's 30 year old character is his identity as a good Muslim man, with a virtuous reputation and respected stature. My friendship with him posed all sorts of challenges and pitfalls for him socially, but also offered opportunities that he could never have anticipated before meeting me.

The prayers finished, and the pair of us sat at a round wooden table in an open space on the edge of the village beneath a shady tree. In the background a water pump, covered by a torn tarpaulin, and surrounded by three men out of earshot from us smoking cigarettes, purred away on its idle. Pure, and absolutely clear, water gurgled its way along the irrigation channels, and Ayoub poured us each a glass of aromatic sweet green tea. 'So what's new, Kasha?' Ayoub asked, looking at me earnestly with his brown eyes.

'I saw Otto yesterday,' I replied, 'he has some information from his friend, the belly dancer, the one from Germany who works in Marrakech, maybe we can make some money, big money.'

Ayoub sipped his tea and nodded.

'You know the family that runs the motorbike shops in Mogador?' I paused for Ayoub to nod again. 'According to the belly dancer, they're looking to expand their business during the Gnaoua Festival.'

'I guess you don't mean legitimate business, brother?'

'No they're looking for good........like really good quality merchandise, the best quality bro, better than that Jbala crap.'

Ayoub sat silently, now no longer looking at me. I could see him checking on the men by the water pump to see if they could hear our conversation. He needn't have worried though, for while his English was pretty competent, there was no chance that the Amazigh villagers would understand a word we were exchanging. After a moment, and now with a twinkle in his eye Ayoub said, 'Big money you say. These motorbike people, this family, they are bad ass you know Kasha….. it will need to be a lot of money to make it worth our while.'

'I'm not saying we should Ayoub, just that Otto has some information that could do us some good,…like really really good. Like life-changing benefits, bro!'

Ayoub drew a slow breath and said, 'In this country Kasha, some people's benefits are like food on a spoon, and other people's benefits are a stick in the eye. I know this family, they are not seeking to help the likes of you and me. How much money are we talking about?'

This was a weighty and fateful moment in our conversation, one that might change our lives. In my heart I had an enthusiasm for Otto's scheme, but I also implicitly trusted Ayoub's understanding of how much jeopardy we might be letting ourselves in for.

'Something like fifty thousand euros.' I replied.

Ayoub was quiet, the diesel-driven pump continued to throb and the sound of splashing water filled the air between us.

'And you think no-one will notice that we have all this new money, even if we're not caught or killed getting it, brother?'

This was the kind of reaction I'd expected from Ayoub, in fact I was glad he was being so circumspect. Becoming involved with the underworld in Morocco should be no whimsical matter, and approached with extreme caution. Just as Alison's advice from her home in the medina yesterday had suggested.

'I only thought you might be interested, that's all....we could always launder the money through a shop in Mogador like Abdul Kaber's or Fiona's cafe,' I said with a touch of optimism in my voice.

'I suppose this is true,' Ayoub acknowledged, 'tell me more about this information from Otto.'

THE BELLY DANCER

Mustaffa used to live on the southern Atlantic coast of Morocco, in a region called the Sahrawi. There he had made a living as a part-time fisherman and general purpose painter for twenty years. He had got married and built a small family home overlooking the sea. Through an indiscretion of the heart, and perhaps some vanity, he ended up getting divorced, with the result that he had to hand over the keys of his house to his wife, and suffer the stigma of a tarnished reputation. Although a few of the local community, mainly his kiff smoking friends, sympathised with the sense of injustice that Mustaffa felt, most of those that knew him thought that he'd got what he deserved. The king's well-educated wife, Salma, had been the driving energy behind the new divorce laws, only fairly recently introduced by the government, and still a source of much discussion and controversy across the country. Mustafa, now in his fifties, was left with a bag of paint brushes, his kiff pipe and a hole in his life where there once was a family and a home. So it was that he returned to live with his widowed mother, Nadjir, in a tiny hilltop village about 20 km from Mogador. There he drifted in and out of occasional painting and fishing work, but mostly spent his time daydreaming, and looking after the chickens and olive trees in his mother's garden.

*****

It was late in the afternoon. Ayoub and I were sat with Mustaffa and his mother, our shoes off, and we were sharing tea and sweet cakes in their front room. Nadjir, whose small tough fingers were smudged with red henna, was complaining about the price of food, and the difficulties of life, especially with a son like Mustaffa. Above where she sat crossed-legged on the floor was a television silently playing an action movie and casting rays of bright light onto the cool dark blue walls of the room. Nadjir finished twisting the last of the dried grass stems that she was knotting into a handle for a basket, got up, rubbed her rheumatic knee, and disappeared out of the open front door leaving the three of us alone.

Ayoub had already had a brief conversation with Mustaffa, where he'd mentioned money and sketched out a little bit of what we were now calling 'Otto's plan'. We were hoping that Mustaffa would be enticed by the offer of several thousand dirhams and be content to get involved, without wanting to know too much about our overall scheme. I could tell straight away though that he was keen to know more, albeit motivated by a base desire, when having checked the doorway he turned to me and in Arabic said, 'This belly dancer that Ayoub mentioned, she is a good one?'

I turned quizzically to Ayoub, pretending that I didn't understand, and hoping that he would steer the conversation away from any lechery that might be fermenting in Mustaffa's mind.

'She's German and reliable,' Ayoub replied with a straight face.

I picked up my glass of hot tea and Ayoub continued, 'She met Aziz Boukh when he was entertaining some Chinese in Marrakech.'

A grin began to form on Mustaffa's lips, 'Entertaining you say, showing them a first-class time you mean?'

Ayoub paused, 'You know of Boukh; leather jacket, tattoos, rich friends in Marrakech with Porsches and expensive tastes. He thinks he is too big for little Mogador, and the motorbike racket his family runs.'

Mustaffa raised his head slightly, inviting Ayoub to continue.

'Well, the belly dancer hears him bragging to the Chinese. He says he's planning to break away from the other Jbala families, and make big profits for himself during the Gnaoua.'

'He has a high opinion of himself, this man,' Mustaffa said. Scratching his chin he continued, 'This sounds like a dangerous thing to become involved with.'

'He's definitely not to be trusted,' I interjected, 'but I think we have a way of helping him to help us, if we are brave,' my Arabic stretching just far enough to make this point.

'It's low risk, but a big opportunity for you,' Ayoub countered. 'The belly dancer has some contact details for Aziz; private details. We use those, he'll take us seriously. If we can get him a sample of some top quality merchandise, european quality, top price stuff, then maybe we can make a deal with him.'

Mustaffa was staring at the floor. With his head bowed he quietly said, 'I need money to make a new start. I don't need trouble or a madman with a machete after me. Mess with Aziz Bourkh you'll get both. Or prison.'

Mustaffa's words hung in the cool, breathless atmosphere of the room for a time, until Ayoub replied, 'These are things for Kasha and me to be concerned with, not you my brother. All we are asking is that you travel north to meet a contact of mine, and bring the sample that he will give you back to us. For these three days of work you will get 3000 dirham and we will ask no more of you. I told you it would be low risk, just a bus ride up to Tamarasque, and then a hire car journey back south. No-one, not even the Macadan will notice you being away.'

'Someone notices everything Ayoub. Don't think I'm so

dumb not to know how life is,' Mustaffa responded, 'but let me think a bit about it a bit.'

THE JBALA NETWORK

Aziz Bourkh was born in the early 1990's, more or less at the same time as the present king stepped up to be the head of state, following his father's death. As the only son of Umar Bourkh, he grew up as the precious and over-indulged heir to the family's growing wealth and reputation in Mogador. Umar had muscled his way to the top of the controlling influences, amongst Mogador's underworld, during the prosperous decades of the new king's reign. A trading and political accord, signed by the king and the Israeli government in 2002 had opened all sorts of economic opportunities for the country, and had been the catalyst for a host of international partnerships. The subsequent investment in the country's infrastructure, the modernisation of its agriculture and the introduction of technology saw an influx of cash and credit flow through the hands of the king and across the country. There then followed a period of internal struggle where competing networks of families vied for power, influence and a slice of the wealth that was being generated. These were families with ancestral claims to land and resources, linked to centuries of sultanate rule. They were well versed in the politics of establishing an agreeable status quo amongst themselves, and letting enough of their prosperity trickle down to the people to keep them ambitious. It was with this economic upturn in the background that Umar Bourkh, and the other four families in Mogador's Jbala network, established control and protection over all business activities in Mogador and its locality. With plenty of cash in circulation it was simple for these families to provide additional funds to the town police, the coastal security, the planning authorities and the powerful elements beyond the town to secure their cooperation. They were also quite capable of extending a storm of violence and trauma to anyone who didn't comply with them or see the virtue in their payoffs, with the result that by the beginning of the 2020's prosperity and progress in Mogador was securely in the pockets of the Jbala network and under the guidance of the family patriarchs, like Umar Bourkh.

From the outside the Bourkh family had a good, if feared, reputation, with residential properties and a complete monopoly on the motorbike trade in Mogador being the backbone of their public wealth. Umar had married a girl from a coastal village south of the town, keeping up his family's conservative respectability. The couple's four children, Aziz being the youngest and only male, had a traditional upbringing without the trappings of a sophisticated education like some of their wealthy contemporaries in the larger, more cosmopolitan cities of the north. Aziz's sisters had each married, and moved out to live in comfortable parts of Mogador's suburbia, while Aziz grew into his thirties still with a bedroom at home. His mother though rarely had to change his bed linen for mostly Aziz slept in hotels under his family's protection, where his predilections and desires could be fulfilled without the family's watchful eye. His friends, although they were more like associates, treated Aziz with some unease, being both excited by his passionate ambition but fearful of his errant attraction to the forbidden. There were graves of men and women in the arid land outside Mogador where those that had fallen foul of Aziz's desires or wishes, had been disappeared. The juicy fruit of prickly pear cacti benefiting from the decaying remains of those with the misfortune to suffer at Aziz's whim. Unlike the king, who'd become a steady, if shy and unremarkable, father to the prospering state, Aziz was an unpredictable and rich narcissist, exploiting his birthright with little concern for others.

Indeed his lack of empathy had recently led to an

acrimonious and potentially serious fall out with his father after a recent 'business' trip to Marrakech. Aziz and his coterie had been entertaining Chinese motorbike merchants in the affluent outskirts of the city with some hazy evening pleasures. Following hours of partying he'd lost control, becoming belligerent about the other ruling families in Mogador, and bombastic about a scheme to wrestle influence from the older generation. The Chinese were neither impressed, nor really understood his outburst, but reports of it seeped back his father, who'd become increasingly uneasy about Aziz's behaviour and reputation. The pair of them had exchanged heated views in the ensuing days, Aziz feeling slightly ashamed and betrayed, while his father was angry, and worried about the hurricane of turmoil his son and heir might be capable of bringing to Mogador.

GECKOS

In front of me the long straight road stretched out into the dry and parched Moroccan landscape. The mid morning air was warm, blown only lightly by the sirocco breeze that would gather intensity as the day wore on. A group of camels stood grazing by the edge of the scrub forest, their front legs tied together, their heads turning to follow me as I buzzed by on my motorbike. I'd got lots on my mind, and an appointment with Alison in Mogador. The periodic appearance of black rubber marks scraped into the tarmac was a good reminder, though, that I needed to be alert. Free-roaming cows, dogs, donkeys, sheep and the like are a camouflaged and deadly hazard on the roads, with the abundance of skid marks and carcasses a testimony to this. I wasn't hurrying. It had become a familiar eventuality that I would be late to my appointments with Alison. I think she was secretly pleased that slowly I was sinking into the charm of Moroccan time keeping and perhaps some of its other sorcery. As I drove by those scrutinising camels, with their big eye lashes and considered gaze, I wondered what they would make of the dream I'd had last night.

*****

I put my keys on the kitchen table of Alison's house, sat down and watched her finish putting bread out on the window ledge for the birds. Bright African sunlight shone into the room, picking the dust out hanging in the air, and wrapping her silhouette in a white veil of energy.

'I love the birds,' she said, 'and how they sing with such happiness. You know, in this country it's considered bad luck to whistle inside your home, but birds can sing all day wherever they are, with all their heart, and not a worry to fear.'

'That's until a cat gets them,' I responded, not really thinking about what I was saying, but almost immediately sensing an enquiring shift in Alison's stance by the window.

'You're a bit edgy today. You got something on your mind?' she said, turning and picking up my keys from the table.

We looked at each other briefly. I opened my mouth to say something, probably out of shame for mentioning the thing about cats, when I noticed her running her finger tip around the edge of the one dirham coin that was now attached to my key fob.

'You have a charm here Kasha, a blessing.'

I didn't say anything. There was no need to explain how I'd come across the coin, or why I'd kept hold of it. Alison, like me, could feel its inanimate potency, its energy bleeding invisibly from the stone ore that it had been cast from and the royal etchings on its surface.

After a moment's stillness, a knowing smile lit up Alison's face, and raising her head slightly she said,

'With this in your pocket you should look out for treasure, Kasha.'

'Yeah, I know, but treasure comes in many disguises and I'm not sure what to look for. That's kind of why I rang. I haven't been sleeping well either. I'm restless, Alison. I get these dreadful dreams where my throat's slit.'

'That's a bit gruesome! You *have* got a lot on your mind, haven't you,' Alison acknowledged as she moved to sit on the window ledge with her back to the sun. 'Make sure there are no geckos in your room at night. They have the breath of Shaitan in them, supposedly from all the way back to the time of Abraham. They'll fill up your dreams with monsters and demons if you let them near you. Bolt your windows closed at night and that will help your dreaming.'

Staring at Alison's outline against the sunshine from the window, with my mouth open in slight disbelief, I took a second or two to process her comments. Was she really expecting me to believe that geckos could be the conduit for demons and fiends? That seemed unlikely. Then again perhaps my unconscious mind might be triggered by the appearance of a scaly reptile, with an elongated body and a fictional role in explaining the existence of evil. Whatever she meant, she was right about the geckos' villainy in relation to Abraham, and with notoriety like that why wouldn't they still be carrying that curse all these millennia later?

I was still mulling this over when she interrupted my thoughts.

'There's a much stronger influence than geckos disrupting your ambience though Kasha, I could tell that well before you mentioned your dreams. Who've you been listening to, not that dodgy German guy, what's his name?'

'Otto,' I answered.

'Yes of course, Otto, that's him. You know he's got a reputation for being zigzag, don't you?'

Alison had handed me my keys back by now, and as I turned the one dirham coin in the palm of my right hand, I caught a glimpse of the royal coat of arms on its reverse side. There, inscribed in Arabic was a Quranic verse. It read, 'Guide us to the straight path.' This wasn't exactly an endorsement of Otto's proposal or his reputation. I closed my hand around the coin, but I could tell Alison knew what had just gone through my head.

'If your fate is to seek this treasure, and Otto is involved, you'd better be able to live with a level of fear that you've only seen in your dreams. He will encourage you to follow a path of peril.'

THE COACH

Mustaffa woke to the rustle and murmur of his mother making her fajar prayers, and the old village cockerel crowing for dawn outside. He was warm in his blanket on the bare wooden bench that served as his bed, and still had half his mind in the sleepy comfort of his dreams. There in the front room, beneath the television set fixed on the wall, his day began with the shadowy light cast from his mother's bedroom and a familiar sense of anxiety in his heart. He had a long day ahead of him.

After black coffee and a quick breakfast of honey, olive oil and bread, Mustaffa set out towards the coastal road, where he planned to catch the CTM bus to Asfi. It was still dark, he wore his worn out brown woollen djellaba with its hood up, and picked his way down the rocky village track taking care not to disturb any stones where a sleepy scorpion or a nesting snake might be tucked away. Giant aloe vera plants lined the path, with their spindly serrated leaves stretching high into the predawn sky. In the distance darkness-warning lights on the hilltop wind turbines flashed. Soon the sun would rise, and their huge turning rotors would glint in the red and orange rays of dawn. Had Mustaffa not fallen on hard times, he might have had a hemar to carry him to the roadside, and been able to slap it on its flank to send it back home. Donkeys, though much maligned, do provide a meagre luxury to those living in the countryside, distinguishing the poor from those who have absolutely nothing. Mustaffa, unfortunately, fell into the category of the latter, hence his slow, painstaking trek to the road, and willingness to make this undoubtedly dangerous trip to Asfi.

The traffic going north through the countryside this early in the morning was thin, with long periods of silence stretching out between passing vehicles. Mustaffa waited by the roadside in the twilight of the new day, the calm air hanging still over the cool landscape. A big heavy truck, piled absurdly high with plastic goods, rolled by on the other side of the road bound for Mogador. The truck left an acrid smell of burnt diesel behind, its lights fading into the distance as it disappeared to the south. It was all quiet again. Time passed slowly. Then, with the sun rising on the horizon to the east, Mustaffa's attention was caught by the sparkle of a windscreen and the tell-tale outline of an approaching coach.

*****

Otto wasn't really a morning type of person, and definitely didn't enjoy the annoyance of catching a bus before sunrise. The CTM coach station in Mogador had been pretty much empty, save for a couple of european backpackers and a cluster of middle class Moroccan families. The cafes nearby were shut, however the smell of baking bread from the French style bakeries in the vicinity had a comforting effect on Otto. It wasn't cold, but in the morning darkness he'd worn a coat and hat, giving him a degree of anonymity amongst the other travellers. The CTM coach service does not run on Moroccan time, so it leaves on schedule and will arrive at its destination according to its timetable. Those that use the service pay a little bit more for this sense of certainty, and for the air conditioning and general comfort. The coaches are cleaner than their cheaper counterparts, and by and large are not used by the poorer working classes. Although Otto's ticket had a seat number, these are not checked or given any credence by travellers, so he took up a place midway down the coach.

Putting his shoulder bag down against the window he shimmied into his seat, and checked the thick roll of cash that was wedged into his trouser pocket. He'd convinced himself a long time ago that his days dealing with the underworld were long since past, but here he was again dabbling in the infamy of illegality. Those long forgotten feelings of fear and thrill coursing through his empty stomach, reminding him of the old days in Thailand and the regrettable hold that Ingrid had over him. The alibi she'd given him, and her manner with the town police, had deflected accusations away from him but that didn't mean he was safe. She knew the truth about his predilection for the young and vulnerable. She had the evidence of his personalised hard drive to hold against him. His interest in the seedy world of sex tourism and exploitation had once been an exciting addiction but was now a source of anxiety and threat.

The last thing he'd wanted to do was spend a cramped day on a bus to Asfi, chaperoning a load of cash, and mixing with the likes of Mustaffa and his kin. There was nothing he could do about it though. Ingrid had leverage on him, and anyway, fingers crossed, his part in today's plan, unlike that of Mustaffa's, didn't involve too much jeopardy. Otto leaned back into his seat trying to relax as the coach pulled away and set off through the dim streets of Mogador.

A smart young Moroccan man came to sit beside him; the cologne on his skin made Otto's nose twitch and just vaguely aroused him. He drifted into some unseemly dreamy thoughts with his head leant on the window until the coach began to slow, and eventually stopped a few kilometres from the town by a dusty country verge.

Otto looked up over the seats in front of him to see Mustaffa picking his way along the aisle to a place a couple seats in front. There was no exchange between them, neither caught each other's eye, that'd been the agreement. Otto was relieved that Mustaffa was obviously taking their business seriously, not wanting to raise any eyebrows amongst those that might report unusual liaisons or suspicious traffic.

HANGING TRAINERS

After an hour or so of trundling through the dry and early morning countryside, the coach pulled up in a small village beside the smoky charcoal stoves of a cafe. A donkey trap sat on the opposite side of the road, an old man sitting with the reins in his hand and his younger wife almost completely concealed in a black burqa beside him. The coach doors opened with a whoosh; a clean shaven man with a satchel over his shoulder climbed aboard. As the engine stirred and the driver crunched his way back up through the gears this figure of authority began checking tickets. Swaying in the aisle, his red tracksuit top, jeans and fake Gucci cap gave him a rather ordinary and low-key appearance. Had Otto not known better he'd have assumed that the inspector was simply checking ticket and traveller numbers to make sure there wasn't any extra undeclared money being earned by the driver and conductor. There was a lot more than just that going on though, for in Morocco nothing happens without someone knowing, and someone else finding out. The flow of every day information from people like this inspector, or the Macadams, made illegal or forbidden activity difficult to say the least. Order and control are maintained through a complicated network of informants providing the state with an insight into potential threats and people making money without the appropriate payoffs. Otto watched, trying to feign lack of interest, as in front of him Mustaffa handed over his ticket and the inspector tore its edge. There was nothing unusual about a man like Mustaffa making a journey north, although had he been doing it regularly then that might have provoked a little bit of interested scrutiny from the likes of this man. Equally it wasn't particularly concerning for the inspector to see Otto with a ticket to Asfi, even if he was a touch older than the normal backpackers who used the service.

*****

Asfi is a city built on several hills overlooking the Atlantic ocean. It has a university, a large medina and a commercial port, from where sardines, agricultural chemicals and its traditional ceramic goods are exported. It has a notorious reputation for gangs and the darker arts, and is not a city with a tradition of welcoming tourists or expats. The CTM coach station is located by the docks, adjacent to the old steam railway line that is still used to shunt materials around the port. There was a distinct whiff of soot in the air as Mustaffa and Otto disembarked and made their separate ways from the coach into the surrounding bustle of shops and amenities.

No-one would suspect there to be any connection between the pair. Indeed Mustaffa slipped invisibly away into the throng of colour and noise while Otto had to deal with the attention of taxi touts and children trying to sell him packets of tissue.

The arrangement was for them to make their own way to the eastern edge of the medina, via the Bab Chaaba gate, where Otto would hand over the cash to Mustaffa, who in turn would swap it for the merchandise from Ayoub's contact. The rendezvous would happen in a cafe located near to some overhead cables from which a pair of trainers would be hanging.

Mustaffa and Otto had just over an hour to make this appointment, and filled their time mingling amongst the late morning shoppers, blending quietly into the general babble and din. Otto bought a couple of chocolate patisseries which the confectioner put in a white card box and wrapped it with a ribbon. Discreetly Otto squeezed the 1000 dirhams into the box, knowing that such an item would raise no eyebrows if it was sitting appetisingly on a cafe table. He could smell the rich chocolate cakes in his hand, as he spied the hanging trainers swinging in the breeze a street or two away.

Mustaffa was loitering by a clothes shop, rummaging through the packs of socks and branded sportswear displayed in plastic crates on the narrow medina street. Otto brushed past him, placed the cake box on the piles of socks and disappeared into the shop. Mustaffa picked up the box, and went to order a coffee in the cafe beneath the trainers.

The transaction in the cafe had all gone to plan. Mustaffa had finished his coffee, paid, and then left the establishment with a matching but much heavier white cake box, minus, of course, the 1000dh.

'What if this is a set-up,' he thought, his heart quickening in the medina street. 'Might there be plain clothes police waiting to pounce. My life would change. No more living free in the countryside. I'd be in a stinking prison cell, sleeping in filth and never feeling the wind on my face.'

Mustaffa had half the 3000 dirham that Ayoub had promised him, but right at this moment that didn't seem nearly enough to cover the prospect of jail if he was caught with the box and its forbidden contents.

'BisMillah,' he said to himself, inwardly cringing at the prospect of having to eat fish heads and scrape maggots from the prison floor where he might spend his days.

He needed this break though, the money would get him out of his mother's house and onto his own feet again. Mustaffa tried to reassure himself. He knew Hussain, Ayoub's contact, had just made twice as much 'floos' as he'd normally make, and there was the promise of an even bigger pay day in the future. So Hussain wasn't going to be doing any informing. If he did speak about what had just taken place he'd have some tricky explaining to do to the traffickers. And Ayoub too. With this in mind Mustaffa felt a little more at ease.

'Inshallah,' he whispered out loud. All that was left for him to do was to meet up with Otto at the hire car depot. From there they'd drive back to Mogador under the guise of a German tourist on a sightseeing tour. A private hire car travelling through the countryside, with a european sat on the back seat, wouldn't raise any suspicions, and he was certain the Mogador town police would wave them through the checkpoint with all the other evening tourist traffic. Everything seemed to have worked out.

KASHA KERMOULD

FLAKY SKIN

I met Otto by the beach in Mogador the morning after he and Mustaffa had driven back from Asfi. He was sat cross legged on the low sea wall, sporting a Bavarian-style cloth hat, a yellow and orange checked shirt and a pair of khaki cotton shorts. As I approached him he looked every bit an elderly German tourist, enjoying a legitimate retirement as he wistfully stared out across the bay. Nearby a spattering of sun-seeking European tourists lounged beneath bamboo shades, periodically fending off Moroccan and Senegalese men selling coffee and cheap sunglasses. Otto was entirely familiar with this beach-side scene, which he'd witnessed and grown fond of over the years. The big hotels on the esplanade provided an almost endless stream of rich, foreign holiday makers, who would enjoy the exotic north African culture from the safe distance of their resorts, and return home after a fortnight with a suntan and a few overpriced trinkets from the medina. Otto was neither rich, nor a tourist, having arrived and set up home in Morocco several years ago, and survived on the pennies of his meagre state pension. He did, however, fit in perfectly to the all white ambience of the beach side cafes and bars, and as such would not be raising any suspicion or interest from Moroccan officialdom. Hopping over the sea wall I sat down beside him and together we watched a weathered trawler in the distance chug its way into the harbour, the faint squawking of gulls that followed it being the only sound between us.

We sat for a while. Nothing was said, and just for a moment I began to worry that something had gone wrong. Perhaps the deal in Asfi had fallen through, maybe Otto and Mustaffa had been betrayed and had spent the night in jail. This wasn't possible because Otto had messaged me last night, I knew they got back safely with the merchandise. Otto's demeanour though was definitely subdued. At last turning to me, he let out a big sigh and said, 'This isn't the business for me anymore, my nerves are shot Kasha. I'm too old, too frail and sketchy to go to prison.'

I left what we'd said hanging in the space between us, just long enough for him to see I was taking him seriously.

'You're not going to jail bro, you're safe. You did good. Getting in and out of Asfi with all that cash, and then the gear, not easy! You've still got what it takes bro.'

Otto twisted slightly on the wall, pulled a packet of Gauloises from the top pocket of his shirt and lit a cigarette. 'Safe? Safely locked up you mean. I didn't think I was going to make it yesterday.'

'What do you mean?' I asked. 'You said Ayoub's contact, what's his name.... Hussain, had sorted everything.'

'Yeah, that was all fine Kasha, it was the journey back south to Mogador that was freaky.' Agitated as he relived the moment, his voice rising, Otto rubbed the flaky skin on his neck. 'I mean the gear was wrapped up in about 20 layers of cellophane but it still stunk. Honestly it reeked. It made me want to be sick. I sat in the back of that car sweating my ass off, scared shitless.... thinking, what the hell am I doing.'

Checking the beach nearby I shushed him, 'Not so loud Otto, the walls have ears!'

Otto tossed his dying cigarette butt into the sand in front of us, tipped his head and continued, 'The gendarme check point, where the coastal road cuts inland to meet the main drag from Marrakech to Mogador. You know, a couple of kilometres from El-Sheba, that was the worst. I thought we were busted.'

I raised an eyebrow to encourage him.

'Mustaffa saw the queue of traffic first, told me to act casual, with a book or something. That just made it worse. All I could focus on was the gendarmes and their guns. It was hard to keep breathing. Anyway, we're on a downhill, there's a truck and a bus in front, and it feels like it's only a matter of time before we're in shit. It was madness. I'm sitting in a car stinking of contraband, watching a gendarme with Raybans and a whistle walking towards us. There were two sniffer dogs, Kasha. Not good, not good for an old man like me.'

I'd hoped, unrealistically as it transpired, that Mustaffa and Otto would have a clear run all the way back to Mogador, but had suspected they might encounter such a gendarme road block. Otto had a lot of extra cash on him to pay for this kind of eventuality, but this would be a very unfavourable outcome. The gendarmes would relieve us of our much needed money, they'd become aware of Otto and Mustaffa as people moving illegal merchandise, and with those kinds of connections they'd both be watched by the authorities intently.

'The sniffer dogs?' I enquired.

'Yup, two German shepherds, ironic really eh,' Otto answered. 'We had to wait while they searched the potato truck and then the bus. After that they waved everyone else though. I daren't look back in case they changed their minds and wanted to search us.'

'They were most likely doing random checks, you think?'

'Yes, if they'd had information they would have found something, and if we'd been informed on, they'd have got us for half a kilo and ten thousand dirham,' his head dipping as he relived the panic and angst from that moment. He bit his finger nails, rubbed the weathered skin on the back of his hand that I knew he shaved, and replied to me in German. This was a habit of his, mostly when he was at ease but occasionally triggered by a surprise or apprehension.

I waited quietly, he realised and said in English, 'Ingrid wants to meet with you, give me a lift home and you can pick up the gear.'

KHAMSA

'You know she's spelt 'Hamsa' wrong, don't you,' Ayoub commented as we both stood looking at the big blue door to Fiona's workshop.

The slender, three storey building, nestled in a narrow Mogador street had formerly been the home of a widow called Fatima, so its association with this abrahamic symbol of protection wasn't entirely out of keeping. The pair of us had met an hour earlier for a breakfast coffee in the medina, to catch up and make preparations for our imminent meeting with Aziz Bourkh. 'I think adding the K is optional,' I replied unconvincingly.

Ayoub shook his head, and leant against the whitewashed wall opposite the house, with his motorbike helmet resting on his knee. Exhaling as he studied the blue door and the golden Hamsa lettering painted above it, I could tell he was unimpressed.

'Why do you try to find a way to excuse her, Kasha? I told you what I think. When she was young she got everything she wanted, now she's old with money she makes everything as she wants it. She likes you because you are nice, you're friendly, and you listen. She doesn't want you as a man Kasha, you've told me this. Everyone in the medina knows she likes girls, in fact everyone in Mogador has heard about this silver-haired English woman. How do you think I know about her?'

I looked at Ayoub. It was true that the rumour mill from the medina could spill its tawdry gossip far and wide, and that Fiona had a reputation. This of course might have been borne from jealousy, a very common emotional currency in the makeup of the Moroccan psyche, but there was more than a grain of truth to these suspicions. Whilst many in Morocco may lack sophistication they certainly have an uncanny insight into the heart and motives of others. It would be folly to disregard their general conclusions about someone, even if their assessment was motivated by envy.

'She's useful, brother,' I pushed back at Ayoub. 'Firstly, she has many female acquaintances, which I would have thought would appeal to you. Spending a little time around this workshop might lead to all sorts of possibilities my friend.'

Ayoub stared back at me with his brown scrutinising eyes, and remained unimpressed, 'The girls coming here to paint or cook, or do whatever, are not interested in a man like me, Kasha. I mean come on!'

'Okay, I'll give you that,' I acknowledged, 'but she's going to be really useful to you and me as cover, when we go north to score.'

Ayoub almost smiled, and prising himself from the wall, he set off to his right down the narrow cobbled street. I followed, enjoying the warmth of the early morning sun on my skin as it heated the cool medina shadows. Catching up with him he continued, 'I'm glad you're thinking that far ahead, she's not going to take some of our cut though is she?'

This time I smiled because I knew he'd like what I had to say, but before I'd gathered my breath to reply he added,

'Oh and I'm looking forward to hearing how you think a rich white European woman is going to give you and me cover. She's more likely to attract attention. In a place like the Rif we'll stand out like a snake on the road. You better have a good plan.'

'It's in hand bro,' I returned, negotiating my path through a throng of Israeli tourists and their guide. 'She's in Marrakech this week, checking out a source of hers. She reckons they've got hold of some antiquities, furniture and ornamental things, that have been shut up in some dark forgotten home and are going to be worth a fortune. It's her new thing.'

Behind us we heard the rattle of an old luggage barrow approaching, with a gaggle of holidaymakers in tow following their bags. As it edged its way past us we cut left, dipped our heads under a low archway, and emerged in the empty passageway that runs throughout the medina immediately inside the fortified walls. The passage isn't a secret but is not frequented by foreigners, mostly because it's off the beaten track and there is no shopping.

'She doesn't need any money Ayoub, and anyway I'm not going to tell her about what we're up to until the very last moment, or even ever,' I continued, letting my left hand brush against the rough and cold stone of the passageway. 'She's driven up to Marrakech in that mini van of hers, you know the posh Merc she bought. That thing will be perfect for us if I can talk her into going North to Tetouan on an antiques run.'

'Oh well, I'll leave that with you Mr Kasha, she's your friend not mine, and anyway I've got our meeting with Aziz on my mind. That better go well, otherwise the whole thing's off anyway!'

I grunted back at Ayoub, inwardly contemplating the many variables that stood in the way of our plan.

Side by side we emerged from the dinghy light of the passageway, squinting for a moment in the sunshine at Bab Spa, the southern gateway to the medina. We shook hands, and made our way over to where the motorbikes were parked.

'That girl from the bakery will keep your mind off Aziz for a bit, you going to take her out of town?' I asked, wrapping my scarf over my face before slipping my helmet on.

'Yeah, sitting together looking at the ocean, without any worries, got to be better than hiding away at the back of some cafe in Mogador.'

He was right, the pair of them would be much more at ease away from the prying eyes of interested friends or relations who might see them in Mogador. 'She has beautiful eyes bro, but I don't envy you,' I said, winking at him as I started my engine.

'It all just depends on your perspective Kasha, kind of like the spelling of Hamsa really,' Ayoub replied.

Then, dropping his bike into gear, and with a growl of acceleration he disappeared into the new town traffic, knowing that the next time we met we'd be on the way to cut a deal with Aziz Bourkh.

TALES FROM MOGADOR: KASHA AND THE KIFF

FINANCIALS

It was mid morning. I'd shared breakfast with Fiona, showered and was just applying some black charcoal Kohl to my eyes when a dark furrow on my brow caught my attention in the mirror. The Twarq desert nomads who use Kohl to protect their eyes would never have concerned themselves with such vanity but I didn't like the furrow. It could've been the result of age but it wasn't. It was anxiety. I was apprehensive about meeting Aziz Bourkh.

There were a lot of reasons why he wouldn't be interested in dealing with a foreigner like me, even with my credible local reputation and ability to speak Arabic. He was most comfortable with the language of paranoia, vanity and ruthlessness, and he was fluent in these. He probably didn't know it but in many respects he'd cultivated a character that was perfectly in tune with the ancient tradition and ancestry of Moroccan outlaws. His vicious and suspicious nature establishing him as a notorious and feared gangster, at ease with cutting the throats of those he didn't trust, and leaving their bodies for rats and roadside dogs to eat.

Unsurprisingly then the only motive that Aziz would have to listen to me and Ayoub, and buy the merchandise we had to offer, was one of pure self interest. This being so, the quality of our product and its likely profitability had to be indisputable, so pausing to sit in Fiona's studio I rehearsed the figures in my mind once again. We'd buy the merchandise from Ayoub's trafficking contact, a friend he'd met in an Algerian prison, for 2 dirhams a gram, that'd cost us 120,000 dirham for the 60kg. It'd be top quality merchandise, being the first batch of pollen that the Rif farmers would beat from the kiff, usually exported through criminal channels into Europe for the best price. This kind of high grade material would fetch an eye watering €7 a gram in places like the UK or Germany, which translated into a ratio of over 700 dirhams a gram. The huge profit margins were clear to see, but not normally available to the dealers in Morocco. Their clientele was from a much poorer demography, and so with less cash to spend the merchandise sold inside the country was lower in quality and from the second or third processing of the kiff.

In towns like Mogador dealers would be selling the second grade product for at best 10 dirhams a gram to tourists or foreigners, and to the locals for perhaps 5 dirham. Ayoub and I were going to be offering 60 kg of top grade, European standard product, to Aziz for the nominal fee of 10 dirhams a gram, making a total of 600,000 dirham. We'd be walking away with a profit of over €50,000 whilst Aziz, who would corner the market with our premier product could potentially turn his outlay into something around 1.2 million dirham or over €120,000.

In addition to the increased revenue, there'd be the prestige and prominence Aziz would gain from taking control of the market, and the opportunities that might arise from supplying wealthy foreign visitors to the Gnaoua festival with the best product Morocco could offer. The time seemed right, the omens so to speak appeared to be aligned.

I knew Aziz was ambitious, Ayoub had reliable contacts in the Rif and trafficking cabal, Otto and Ingrid had stumped up the first load of expenses and Mustaffa had fetched the half kilo sample from Asfi. I still felt apprehensive about meeting Aziz though. Once we'd initiated the wheels of this drug smuggling scheme, there'd be no going back. No more living anonymously as a foreigner in this sunny and fascinating west African nation. We'd all be on Aziz's radar for ever more. It was therefore imperative that if Aziz did accept the terms of our proposed deal, and was suitably impressed with the quality of our sample, that the business of buying and then delivering the merchandise went smoothly.

There were innumerable things that could go wrong with our plan but as long as we didn't do anything to rile or slight Aziz and his associates, we'd have a safe place to continue to call home at the end of it all. Circumstances would be different though, you don't go into business with someone like Aziz Bourkh without there being some leftovers at the end of the day. Aziz would always have information on us that could be of harm and that would definitely give him leverage over us in the future. There was however a lot of money to be made, and by being brave we'd all get a good slice of it. Equally, we'd be useful to Aziz, who in turn might command more authority in Mogador and be able to open further doors of opportunity. Everything could turn out very well, which would be a double relief to Ingrid, whose baby brother desperately needed to pay off the mafia in Malaga, and who'd put herself at risk by recommending Ayoub and me to Aziz in the first place.

I checked the mirror again for that furrow, but it was still there.

TALES FROM MOGADOR: KASHA AND THE KIFF

SOUSA

Fatima had lived in the apartment block next to Ayoub's in Sousa, a busy working class district of Mogador, for as long as he could remember. As a tall, slender Moroccan woman, missing a front tooth and in her fifties, she always dressed in a traditional long kaftan and headscarf, and carried herself with presence. Fairly recently divorced she earned a living through letting the spare apartments in the block she'd been granted in her settlement, and passed her time being obsessively sad that her son had moved out to live with his wife, who she hated. I had briefly rented one of her small flats some time ago, remarking that she'd begun to wear eye liner after I moved in. Ayoub had been dismissive of my observation until he too had noticed, and forevermore Fatima became an endearing character in our conversations. Ayoub jumped over the low wall that separated Fatima's roof terrace from that of his own, and fished out the package that he'd tucked away among the broken parts of a disused pigeon coup. Fatima's previous husband had built the coup, which was now in disrepair. It did however serve as a perfectly secret place to leave the contraband that Mustaffa had brought down from Asfi. As he checked the contents of the package, Ayoub heard the toot of a motorbike horn, and peeping over the edge of the flat top roof he saw me looking back at him from the street below. Skipping down the dark gloomy stairway of his own apartment block, he grabbed his helmet, kissed his mother goodbye and went to join me with the package in a bag on his back.

Sousa is a busy district, with interconnecting residential streets and a vibrant array of small shops selling food and domestic goods. The owners of these shops typically live with their families and relatives above them, and the three storey concrete buildings cast welcome shade from the hot sun. Spilling into its roads are fruit barrows piled high with fresh bananas and oranges, beside which are sleepy Moroccan men and also the remains of sardines and other sea creatures rotting in the kerbside.

Ayoub tapped my helmet with his hand, and we pulled away into the midday traffic. It annoyed Ayoub that I didn't use the indicators on my bike, although he did have to admit that it didn't make much difference. The cars, buses, trucks and horse drawn buggies of the town all negotiated each other in a benign chaos, where accidents were relatively unusual, it being errant dogs that most often fell foul of the traffic. In such an environment the complicated junction near the bus station had to be approached carefully, especially in view of what Ayoub had in the bag on his back. Nevertheless, and even without indicating, we manoeuvred our way past the bus station melee and into the dilapidated atmosphere of the industrial district. It had rained last night, and the sewers in this part of the town, being just a stone's throw from the sea, were backed up. I picked my way slowly through the dirty puddles that lay oily and smelly between all the open workshops. Blacksmiths, mechanics, electricians and cabinet makers had moved into this area that was once dominated by the fishing industry. The derelict buildings that had formerly processed huge quantities of fish were being repurposed by tradesmen, who'd reinvented this part of Mogador after the collapse of the local fish stocks. In these streets Aziz Bourkh was the dominant force, using the old warehouses to store imported goods which were the fruit of his laundered money, and the seclusion of the area to conduct unsavoury business that needed to be done discreetly.

I drove the motorbike up onto the roadside, and stopped near the carcass of a stripped down old Renault 11. The sun was still pretty high in the afternoon sky, and there was a pungent, unpleasant smell in the air. Ayoub slipped off the back of the bike, and without saying anything to me disappeared into the workshop immediately in front of where we'd parked. A moment or two later he re-emerged, and shaking his head said, 'It's somewhere round here. These guys in here don't know, I'm going to try next door.'

Ayoub proceeded to visit several of the workshops in the vicinity, but none of them had any information they could share with him about Aziz's whereabouts. I was beginning to think that either we'd had come to the wrong place or we weren't going to be in luck because no one was prepared to talk about Aziz.

Eventually there was only one place left to try. An unlikely looking building, with shuttered windows on the second and third floors, and a large arched gateway sealed off with big wooden gates. I had taken my helmet off by now, and watched while my rather dejected friend approached and knocked on the entrance door cut into the sturdy wooden gates.

Nothing happened for a moment. Ayoub stood facing the door and waited. My heart quickened in anticipation. Ayoub was going to knock again, but the door moved and then opened just a tiny bit, just enough for whoever was on the other side to see Ayoub.

TALES FROM MOGADOR: KASHA AND THE KIFF

AZIZ

'This is it......come,' Ayoub had said to me as he stepped through the entrance door and disappeared from sight.

Taking a deep breath I put my hand on the edge of the doorway, stepped across the threshold, and found myself standing shoulder to shoulder with Ayoub, facing an unusually burly Moroccan man. No hand shakes, no smiles.

The man before us had a moustache, and was dressed in a faded shirt and worn black jeans. He didn't say anything. Behind him was a square cobblestone courtyard, open to the sky, whose far wall had been knocked through and replaced with rolling steel doors that revealed a shadowy warehouse space beyond. The courtyard contained what looked like a lorry-load of wooden crates, and was noisy with the sound of splitting wood and Arabic banter.

Ayoub glanced at me, pulled the bag from his back and was about to open it when the man in front of us reached out and grabbed it from him. I took a step back. The door out into the street was closed; the men unpacking the crates stopped and stared in our direction. The courtyard was quiet now. Mr Moustache unzipped Ayoub's bag, looked inside, paused, and then without a word motioned with the bag in his hand that we should follow him. I fell in behind Ayoub.

The workmen lost interest in us, got busy with their crates again, and as we climbed the rusty spiral staircase that led up to the balcony I felt a cooling breeze on the back of my neck.

At the top of the staircase we were greeted by a well-groomed and much better-dressed man. He exchanged greetings with us both, took hold of Ayoub's bag and leaving Mr Moustache behind, led us along the balcony. Passing a lump of stained wood with a machete sticking out of it and a shackle screwed to its top surface, we made our way through some open French windows and into a large room.

Our well-heeled guide stretched out his right arm to stop us from going any further, avoiding us interrupting what was obviously a heated conversation between a man, who looked like the boss sat behind a big desk and his minion.

The air in the room was decidedly cooler, and a shiver went up my back.

To our left there was a long mirror, on the far wall a row of low soft bench seats covered in colourfully ornate fabric and beneath our feet the woollen patterns of an expensive Persian carpet.

The boss, who I presumed was Aziz, was smoking a cigarette whilst questioning the man standing before him on the other side of the desk. 'What do you mean he killed her,' he barked, blowing smoke into the air, 'How?'

The man opposite Aziz shifted awkwardly on his feet, his gnarly toes fidgeting in his flip-flops, 'He beat her with a gym weight. I don't think he really meant to kill her, but he did. Her mother called the police, they've taken the body and Youseff has run off to hide. I think he's gone to the old ruins in the dunes by Skalla.'

Ayoub and I stood still. This was serious business we'd walked into.

'I'll give the police a call, and sort this out with them,' Aziz muttered, squashing his cigarette butt into an ashtray. 'These young village boys that you get working for me, they can't expect their wives to behave like their mothers. We can't have any more of this, Abdul. It's bad for our reputation, it's bad for my nerves! What are the men saying in the garage?'

Aziz looked up from his desk, and Abdul drew a finger across his throat, 'They're saying their wives want blood, that Youseff was beating her regularly and that no one did anything.'

I could sense anger brewing in Aziz, and just at this point he looked at us. 'Mohamed, what are these two doing here? Who is this foreigner?'

Our guide fiddled with the ring on his right hand, looked at us, looked back at Aziz, and replied, 'They said they had an appointment, something to do with that belly dancer from Marrakech.'

I watched our guide swallow, and wondered how fearful I ought to be. Aziz stood up, and taking a number of steps towards us responded, 'Oh the belly dancer and her gang of smugglers. Ingrid, yes I remember. So you know her.' He took a step towards us. 'So what do you have for me, Mr Ayoub? I hope this foreigner has nothing to do with your smuggling, he won't last long.'

I kept my mouth shut and tried to steady my breathing.

Ayoub took his bag from the man who we now knew was called Mohamed, removed the package of merchandise and offered it to Aziz.

'Not to me,' Aziz snapped, raising his hands, 'give it to Abdul, he'll test the quality. If it's as Ingrid promised, then the deal's good, if it isn't, then there's no deal.'

Aziz swivelled to face Abdul, 'Let me know what you think of this gear, we need the best European quality to sell at the Gnaoua, only the best..... if these guys have the best then we're doing business with them.

'Oh, and handle the matter with Youseff. I don't want to see him or hear about him again, everyone needs to know he's buried face down in the sand. And you,' Aziz continued, turning to face Ayoub and me, 'if you mess me around, just be warned by what you hear happens to this man Youseff. I'll cut your feet and hands off, and feed them to the dogs on the beach.

'You understand?'

A PHIAL OF POTION

'Je ne cherche pas de femme,' was what I eventually had to tell Souad.

It'd been the second time I'd visited the cafe in El-Sheba that she and her mother ran, and my presence was attracting attention in a place that hosted almost no foreigners. Situated in the centre of this rural and dusty town, Souad's cafe overlooked the crossroads where traffic for Mogador or Marrakech would pass, and villagers would park their donkeys, pony traps and battered old vehicles. Souad and her mother did good business, serving honey crepes, chicken and chips, and sweet Bedouin tea, to the steady flow of Moroccan travellers and farmers who stopped for refreshments.

Beside the cafe were two hanoots that the women also staffed, one full of colourful ceramics that were seconds from a factory in Asfi and other selling plastic fittings and furniture. They were busy women. Souad's mother had recently got married to a man some fifteen years younger than her called Malik. He owned a red Fiat car that he parked in the dirt by the broken kerbstones outside the cafe. His days were spent milling around the cafe, and shuttling Souad's two young children to and from school.

Souad had introduced her son and daughter to me on my first visit to the cafe, and although there was only a limited overlap in our shared knowledge of French and Arabic she managed to explain that she was divorced. My second visit to Souad's cafe coincided with the arrival of a couple of her female friends, who, dressed in their ankle length and loose fitting Kaftans and hijabs, soon began quizzing Souad about the foreigner in her cafe.

Under obvious scrutiny from the women, and feeling a little uncomfortable, I had engaged them in conversation as best I could. Amongst the women who'd come to sit under the canopy near me though, there was whispering, nudging and mischievous smiles. The fact that I'd returned to Souad's cafe for a second visit seemed to have triggered intense speculation among the women. I could quite clearly see that Souad was enjoying the intrigue, smiling with her friends and casting her brown eyes upon me.

Time passed. Souad's friends finished their gossiping, each one making fond farewells and discreet glances in my direction. When the moment for my departure arrived, Souad attempted to exchange phone numbers with me, to which I feigned misunderstanding. I told her I wasn't looking for a wife and set off on my way. She'd waved me off and let me go, but this wasn't going to be the last of it.

*****

Over the following weeks and months, through Ramadan and beyond, I had continued to visit the cafe in El-Sheba. These had been fun and interesting episodes, but they'd also been opportunities for Souad to affect the course of my fate.

Hidden safely from the prying fingers of her children, on a small shelf beside her gas cooking stove, was a tiny glass bottle of potion, tucked away ready for my visits. On each occasion that she made Bedouin tea she added a drop or two of the elixir to my drink, trusting that the mixture would change my mind and open my heart to her.

Such practices were not uncommon in the rural circles of women that Souad and her mother moved in, the power and influence of sorcery having existed for as long as they and their ancestors could remember. For some reason though the potion did not produce quite the desired effect, and whilst I made regular trips to the cafe in Had-Dra I was often accompanied by foreign women, who I introduced as my friends.

This was not what Souad had planned or hoped for. She put curses on these women, continued to secretly ply me with her potion and decided upon an additional strategy to prise open my heart.

Now whenever I was around, and the chance presented itself, Souad would drape herself over the shoulders of available young men drinking tea in her cafe. Making sure that I was within earshot and could see what she was up to, she'd laugh and play with these men, being provocative in the hope of arousing me.

Her strategy didn't work though. Gossip and innuendo about her conduct spread through the town damaging her reputation, and eventually her patience ran out. Seeking a much stronger allure, Souad acquired a trinket through her mother's village contacts, which was blessed and made magical by a Jebbar. The person in possession of the trinket, a one dirham coin, would be susceptible to suggestion and easily manipulated. Souad hoped that using the trinket would only be a short term strategy, and that once my heart had been suitably touched, she could do away with the thing. It did, however, come with some side effects for me, in the form of bad dreams and restlessness at night. Souad reasoned that this might actually turn out in her favour. If things developed between us and she could dispense with the trinket, she could then remind me how well I was sleeping now that we were together.

All she needed to do was place the one dirham coin in a place where I'd find it without any suspicion.

TALES FROM MOGADOR: KASHA AND THE KIFF

HILAL

From the coastal road, the fishing village of Hilal stands out as a crescent moon shaped sandy bay, with a mosque and its minaret almost touching the ocean on the headland. Near to the turnoff, from which you plunge 300 ft down a winding and crumbly road to the bay, there are the ruins of a Moorish fortress. This was the landmark that Alison told me to look out for.

It was very early in the morning, prayers had only just been said and the sun was still painting the sky with orange, red and yellow light. The fish market, held every Friday in the purpose built concrete facilities, attracted merchants from up and down the coast and opened for business at the break of dawn. Subsequently there was a line of parked vans and trucks on the sandy verge, that I had to negotiate as I picked my way down to the beach and its amenities.

Hilal is located midway between Moulay and Mogador, and is the last remaining fishing village in the area with an independent fleet of small family-owned boats. Moored on the beach, the blue timber carvel vessels land mainly sardines and anchovies, providing a good living for the captains and their crew, and a vibrant seafaring atmosphere of commerce. As such it has lured enterprising Moroccans like Alison's husband, with the means and contacts, into building picturesque villas and holiday retreats near the village, adding even more dynamism to the area.

I parked up, and walked towards the row of sea facing cafes, painted in whitewash but faded and blasted by the wind, and half finished with rebar poking out of their roofs. These buildings were a bit of a shambles, though quite busy on this Friday morning, with their charcoal stoves burning and tables set out under the open sky. I caught Alison's eye, her head scarf blowing in the breeze, and ordering a nous-nous coffee I sat down beside her.

'It's lovely to see you Kasha,' she said above the hubbub of fisher chat and the purr of surf on the shoreline. 'Nice wheels,' she continued with a grin, 'is that Fiona's Mercedes?'

I ignored her question partly because I knew she was teasing me but mostly out of being distracted and tired from last night's restless sleep. I smiled as a silent reply, put my things on the table between us and watched some men untwist their nets in the sea breeze.

'You're tired eh, still having those bad dreams? I hope you're going to be able to drive me safely back to Mogador?'

Alison was all questions this morning. I suspected that she already knew the answers, so I smiled again and asked my own, 'How long's Yahia been building out here?'

'Oh he's had land out here for years, in fact I think he inherited it. There was the usual family tussle over ownership that held things up for a while, but this year he sold half a hectare to a sand merchant and has used the money to start building. I've come out fairly regularly with him to visit the fish market but the trucks have torn up the road so much that the buses won't drive down here anymore.....hence my need for a lift home, hope you don't mind.'

'It's a pleasure to see you Alison, you know that,' I responded, taking a sip of the strong rich coffee that had now arrived. 'I had to go into Mogador anyway, the motorbike's getting an oil change, I've got Fiona's keys so we've got a luxury ride back to Mogador.'

A tiny smirk flickered in the corner of Alison's mouth, 'You don't think she's the cause of your sleepless nights do you?' she probed, almost winking as she spoke.

'She's not been in my bed,' I said with a sigh. 'It's the dreams that are throwing me in turmoil, I just don't seem to be able to rest.'

A stillness settled between us, Alison seemingly in thought. A group of scruffy cats gathered by the smelly plastic bag of fish by her feet. In the background Arab voices, shouts and whistles wafted on the wind from the market, vehicles were being filled and beginning to leave.

'Maybe there is a blessing you can say before you go to sleep that might help. I know a shuwaf who, for a small fee, will make you an incantation, just a few lines to recite each evening to ward off dream demons. The locals believe it works, perhaps it might be worth a try?'

'I don't think that's really what I need, but maybe I'll give it a go, let's see how the next few days pan out. I'm probably more wound up with all that business to do with Otto...... you remember?

'Yes,' she quickly replied with a pointed finger, 'business that you shouldn't be dabbling in.'

I bit my lower lip, she was right but there was no going back now the deal had been sealed with Aziz. I studied two fishermen who were sanding the upturned hull of a boat a few metres in front of the cafe. I couldn't be sure but perhaps they were the cousins Mustaffa had told me about. I didn't say anything in reply to Alison.

Time passed, we finished our drinks and padded our way along the sandy track to where the Merc was parked. Starting the engine with Alison sitting in the passenger seat, and her fish already beginning to smell, I reminded myself to remove my key ring from Fiona's fob. I'd put it there for safekeeping when I'd left my bike at the garage, and it wouldn't do for her to be wandering around with it.

AN UNEASY ALLIANCE

Morocco is a country divided into an inside, and an outside. The land and coastline to the west of the Atlas Mountains, and the range of the northern Rif peaks, is the territory ruled and controlled by the present King. His ancestors, despite historical assaults by the Portuguese, Spanish and Turks, have maintained authority in these lands for the past 500 years as descendants of the prophet Mohamed and Sultans with absolute power. The royal court and its dynasty is immensely wealthy. It commands respect from its citizens through the fear it nurtures; visibly in its public institutions of control, and out of sight through bribery, informing and nepotism. Although there are rich, fertile oases to the east of the Atlas and Rif, much of this territory is challenging to navigate, and populated by tribal people who whilst being subdued, do not feel allegiance to the monarchy. In many respects these mountainous areas, whose notional capital is Fez, are lawless and exist in a mutually beneficial allegiance with the Moroccan monarchy. On either side of the mountain divide there is a legacy of violence and brutal behaviour. The King's forces of control are well armed but equally so are the peasant farmers from the mountains, both of whom are well aware of their descendents' pleasure in macabre bloodletting, like that of beheading and disembowelling. At present a truce, based on reciprocal economic reward and non-interference, exists between the inside and outside of Morocco, but this arrangement is always in a state of flux with neither those from the kingdom nor the mountain tribes trusting each other. In this context it is not surprising that the monarchy has imposed strict controls on the purchase of coastal land by foreigners. The ruling family are well-practised in sustaining authority, and by confining the expat community to a relatively small and designated geographical space near to Ghazoua, some 5km from Mogador, they have kept a firm grip on foreign influence.

*****

Otto was watching a big brown cockroach make its way along the edge of the wall, scuttling in short bursts of energy, under the stools that stood empty against the bar. He hadn't been waiting long at 'Nomad and Friends' when Ingrid arrived in a flurry of loose fitting top, tight jeans and flip flops. He could smell the scent of cat on her, even before she was close enough for him to reach out to take her hand. She was feeling equally repulsed by his smooth, bony touch and the odour of stale cigarettes, as she sat down opposite him. It was midday and the bar was virtually empty. Last week a middle-aged French woman had fatally collapsed on the dance floor and the subsequent turmoil was keeping people away. As such it was a perfect place for Ingrid and Otto to meet, the other licensed bars in the expat conurbation soaking up its clients in their sleazy alcoholic pursuits.'

'You good?' Ingrid asked, sipping what looked like a gin and tonic, leaning back into her chair and crossing her legs.

Otto could see how her beauty and allure would complement her profession but this was not something he was seduced by. And anyway, he was much more preoccupied by the affairs connected with Mustaffa and Kasha. 'Yeah I'm okay,' he replied hesitantly, and then continued, 'Well actually no, I'm not good. I really don't like this thing that you've got me involved with. These people we are dealing with are crooks, they're not to be trusted..... you know what they do to those who cross them Ingrid, you do know don't you?

A meanness fell upon Ingrid, her eyes tightened, she saw Otto as yet another weak, spindly man and waited a second before saying anything. 'You don't need to worry, you're barely involved. I'd almost believe you if you told me you knew nothing of our plan. It's not like you have a choice anyway Otto, I surely don't need to remind you about the business with the orphanage do I?'

Otto's face flushed, his head dropped. He fidgeted, fished out a cigarette and lit it.

Ingrid sat forward and pushed her phone across the table. 'You see that knife?' she hissed, pointing to an image on the phone's screen, 'that's courtesy of the mob in Malaga. The one's that Marek owes money to. I need the cash we're going to make from this deal with Aziz, by the end of Eid Al Hadha and the Gnaoua, that's three weeks Otto. Then it'll all be over and you can go back to your dirty, oh I mean happy, ways.'

Otto hated this woman. Her painted toe nails, her 13 cats and unruly dog, her stupid little baby brother frightened of losing his fingers or something else, and the secret she knew about him. Yeah, he really did hate her, he'd get her back somehow though.

'Ayoub has contacts in El Jadida and the Rif,' he eventually responded, partly to reassure her, but mostly so she didn't mention his furtive pleasures again. 'He's that friend of Kasha's I told you about, works in car rental. He's setting things up but told me they'll need cash to pay off the traffickers and the police.'

'Okay,' Ingrid replied, 'he'll need cash for the 60kg too, but you're only to hand it over to Kasha. We'll never see it again if any of those Moroccans get their hands on it.'

TALES FROM MOGADOR: KASHA AND THE KIFF

PINK LIPSTICK

The wind hummed a tuneless drone across the poles of the steel sunshade, under which Ayoub sat and checked inside his bag. Mogador airport, located 10 km south of the town, was busy this morning, providing Ayoub with plenty of cover and diversion to make his trip to Tangier appear anonymous and everyday. It is a 13 hour journey by road from Mogador to Tangier, but by plane it will only take an hour and a half. Ayoub would be leaving behind him a tell-tale trail in officialdom, but this trip was relatively innocuous. The opportunity to have both a comfortable journey and mix with more urbane Moroccans easily compensated for the unlikely bureaucratic residue he might be leaving behind.

He had a change of clothes, a laptop, his documents and ticket, and the keys to the Merc that Kasha had lent him. He'd parked next to the attendant's hut. This was safely away from harm and the cunning hands of thieves, and would be ready for him when he flew back tomorrow. Something must be going on between those two, he thought, as he stuffed the key fob away, and pushed the velcro together on the small courtesy pocket. He did one last check, making sure he hadn't overlooked anything that might cause suspicion from the zealous airport officials. Bending over the bag to do the top zip up, he heard a woman's voice.

Beside him, out of the glare of the morning sunshine sat a well-dressed, hijab-wearing Moroccan woman, probably a little younger than himself, asking if he had a lighter.

'Thank you,' the woman said, placing the camel cigarette

between her pink lipsticked lips and sparking a flame from the lighter.

Smoking is of course Haram, or forbidden, not something a good Muslim would do. Ayoub, a devotee to the Muslim brotherhood, Allah and The Quran, was however quite partial to the temptation of Haram, finding pleasure an easy temptress. Maybe she was the same?

Even though he didn't approve, he found it intriguing and arousing that this unaccompanied woman was breaking Muslim sharia so publicly. How different from the village or even Mogador girls whose company he was used to. They had to guard their reputation by being secret sinners, making their own peace with Allah at the same time as avoiding the critical scrutiny of their family and neighbours, who'd be quick to pass judgement. A frisson of excitement quivered through his body as the woman leaned towards him, her loose sleeve brushing his bare arm as she passed back the lighter. He was glad he'd done his morning prayers, and not left them til later, his mind now clouded with frustration and desire.

Picking his backpack up, he turned briefly to smile at the woman, and then crossed the small plaza to the airport's entrance. Two sleepy gendarmes sat by the X-ray machine, beckoning the queue of travellers through security with lazy waves of their hands, and half glances up from their phones.

This was the first time Ayoub had flown since his forcible repatriation from Algeria just after the pandemic. This time he was travelling freely, albeit with nefarious intent. An altogether different experience than his maiden flight in handcuffs and shackles, courtesy of the Algerian secret police. He'd renewed his passport and identity papers since then, and having checked-in without any official eyebrows being raised he waited, feeling uncomfortable and out of place, in the sterile departure lounge.

*****

The plane was full. Ayoub had a window seat, felt giddy during the take-off, and was quite unnerved by the plane's flight path over Mogador's prison. Once he'd sorted out the air pressure in his ears and got his breathing back under control, an ease settled upon him, the deep blue ocean crashing silently on the coastline beneath the wings of the plane a soothing tonic.

In the two seats to his left were Moroccan men, wearing European-style business suits and cocooned with their digital devices. Their body language was that of frequent and confident air travellers, as opposed to Ayoub who was almost hypnotised in awe, like a child, by the colours and shape of the coastline far below.

He recognised Moulay and Hilal, and in doing so his mind drifted to Mustaffa, and the cousin who had a fishing boat there. Ayoub could understand why Mustaffa hadn't needed much persuasion to get involved with them. He needed the money, and the opportunity of making fast money was even more appetising. This afternoon, at the docks in Tangier, he'd get Mustaffa's name down on the crew list for the 'Mama Wats.' If Mustaffa was lucky he might even get paid for that bit of work too.

It was the same for Ayoub. He could transform his life with an injection of some capital. Gone would be the long, boring days at the car rental hanoot in the medina. Instead of that he'd be able to buy some land, build his own house, grow food and even raise animals to sell. Such a situation would make a big change to his eligibility and perhaps attract the kind of wife that'd meet his desires.

Far beneath Ayoub, and his musings, the urbanised and coastal outline of Casablanca and then Rabat passed by. The sprawl of these cities eat into the countryside, with their toll roads and high speed railways scratching unnaturally straight lines across the landscape.

The man next to him had undone his shoe laces. Ayoub could smell the man's feet and was disappointed that such habits were allowed on planes. As a distraction to the odour he let his mind wander to Kasha, but with him it wasn't so easy. Kasha's motivation for being in Morocco at all confused Aouyb, let alone him getting wrapped up in a scheme with mortal jeopardy. Kasha was a puzzle indeed.

Ayoub felt the air pressure in the cabin change again. For some reason he thought about the keys to Fiona's Merc, and reached to feel for their profile through the material of his bag. They were there. Touching down with a hurried jolt, the plane came to rest at the domestic flight terminal of Tangiers Ibn-Battouta International airport. It was still only mid-morning. If Hussain was prompt, there'd be all afternoon and evening for he and Ayoub to make arrangements with the traffickers. Then life would be even more dangerous.

KASHA KERMOULD

HUSSAIN

'Salaam alaikum, khoya, how was the flight?' Hussain asked with an outstretched hand as he greeted Ayoub on the concourse outside the terminal building.

The airport complex, located a short drive southeast from the outskirts of Tangier, was immaculately maintained. Its clean lines of design and gleaming window facade, reflecting both the aspirations of an ambitious developing nation, and a row of tall palm trees. Hussain ushered Ayoub towards the Renault van he'd parked nearby, the pair weaving their way through a congestion of taxi touts and tourist agents all jostling for business in the mid morning sunshine.

The van was an inconspicuous grey, versatile and perfectly suited for the kind of criminal activity it was used for. Whispering 'Bismillah,' and bringing the diesel engine to life with a shudder, Hussain pulled out through the exit gates and onto the autoroute to the city.

'It was quick and cheap,' Ayoub had replied, and now, as he wound his passenger seat window down, he said, 'I can hardly believe we have benefits like these cheap air flights Hussain, maybe we should be doing business using them?'

Hussain, looking over the top of his sunglasses at Ayoub, smiled with a chuckle, 'You don't think we already are, brother?'

Ayoub could smell the scent of blossom from the verge-side flower-beds. This was obviously a city that had pride and wanted to impress visitors. Where there was a livelihood to be made in tending flowers by the roadside, there would surely be secret money being made in air freight. Kasha and he would have to explore this avenue some other time, for now he needed to go to the docks and get Mustaffa signed up on the crew list for the Mama Wats. 'I've got lots to learn,' Ayoub replied.

Hussain checked the traffic, and then himself, in the rear view mirror. It wasn't busy. They'd quickly be able to make their way around the perimeter of the city, passing the shantytowns of rural Moroccans and Senegalese migrants, and onto the road north to the container port.

Making plans in his head, Hussain said, 'We can go to Ksar es Majir after the docks. Get some fish or lubea there for lunch, and then meet up with the traffickers from Tetouan. Siad and his brothers have a place in Majir, where you can talk with them without any fear, how does that sound?'

Ayoub nodded, distracted by the mess of plastic and wooden shanty structures that they were driving past. The colourful and rickety chaos, without running water or sewage, was a bridging point for the poor in their quest to find a better life in Tangier. Working in the medina or in other low paid employment in the city, they held dreams of moving into an apartment in the concrete tower blocks of the suburbs. In the meantime though, they eked out an existence on the periphery of this hilly city. It was a gateway to Europe and the Mediterranean for those in commerce or with wealth, but a dusty, dirty, disease-ridden place of insecure residence for the poor. Ayoub didn't have much, but he did have his faith, and Allah was not guiding him in similar footsteps. He may have been poor, but he would never live like the people in these slums.

'Good,' Ayoub replied.

*****

The Mama Wats was a general ocean-going cargo vessel, just over a 100m long and with a normal crew size of 15. For the past two years it had been sailing between North Africa and Mexico, carrying gypsum down from Tangier to Agadir, and then cement from there on to Mexico City. Its Indonesian captain and crew mostly got their employment contracts via online adverts but with the right connections it was also possible to pick up unlicensed work on such vessels through an agency at the port.

Having cleared the inscrutable gaze of the harbour police, who themselves were overshadowed by an army of giant dockside cranes, Hussain drove from the port security gates to the administrative block. Here the sounds of industry echoed against the massive steel hulls of ships tethered with huge chains, and the smell, and stain, of oil hung in the air and underfoot.

Making their way up several sets of stairs, the pair emerged into an open plan area on the third floor, hosting a cafe, several retail outlets and a collection of dimly lit offices. Sitting outside one of these offices, by a sign promoting 'Abdul Mullah - shipping and exports,' Ayoub waited fretfully.

Hussain wasn't long though, the establishment being part of a wider syndicate of influence that he and his family were financially acquainted with. As he left the office and handed Ayoub a brown manila folder, Hussain rather belatedly asked, 'This Mustaffa of yours, he's been to sea before?'

Ayoub took the folder, its contents being Mustaffa's contract and port entry card, and in his most reassuring tone said, 'Yeah, yeah, he was a fisherman down in Sahrawi, it's all good.'

'It is, my brother, everything between us since Algeria is always good,' Hussain responded and then added, 'I can't feed my family with goodness though. I need 1000dh for this clerk I have just paid.'

Ayoub fished out five 200dh notes from his wallet and placed them in the palm of Hussain's left hand. 'We'll square you up for all this help with a kilo, brother. Let's go and see what your friends in Majir have got to offer.'

He stood and shook Hussain's right hand to seal the deal.

AID

'Have you ever thought about what you'd do if there was an earthquake?' I asked, looking at Fiona who was sitting across her kitchen table from me. 'I mean there's some long old cracks in the walls of my home in Moulay, it's made me think, you know?'

It was early afternoon and I'd popped round to Fiona's home, in the ramparts of Mogador's medina, to share some black tea and patisseries. She'd just got back from her workshop, only a short bicycle ride away, where builders had been busy for the past few weeks renovating the basement. The work hadn't gone particularly smoothly. There had been a catalogue of snags, ranging from minor aesthetic disagreements, to days on end when no one arrived for work. She'd employed an English-speaking Moroccan to act as a foreman but I got the impression that this had only made matters more complicated.

'It'd probably depend on where I was,' she replied, wiping a cake crumb from her lip.

'True,' I acknowledged, 'I was lying in my bed an evening or two ago, and couldn't help noticing two huge cracks in the outside wall. I don't know why but I thought about the earthquakes up in the Atlas and Rif mountains last winter, and then imagined what I might do if something similar happened in Moulay.'

Fiona was listening intently. I watched her scan the wall behind me, and followed her gaze to the ceiling above our heads.

I continued, 'I don't think you get much warning with these things. If you're inside, you need to get out quickly. That might be quite tricky here, your stairs down to the street are so steep. In my place it'd be a nightmare. I reckon the walls would buckle and warp, and then the roof would just drop, crushing everything. You'd get so little time to react, you'd have to move like lightning as soon as you felt the quake.'

'Imagine if you had kids, that'd be terrifying,' Fiona chipped in. 'You know, it reminds me that the ex-pat community up in Ghazoua collected a whole pile of relief aid for the survivors of the earthquake. I don't think it was ever sent, you know. Typical of them, plenty of ostentatious behaviour but no substance. I could check, and if it's still there let's make a detour into the mountains, and drop it off when we go up to Tetouan.'

Fiona's suggestion caught me a touch off guard, for whilst I was hugely keen to persuade her into going north, I didn't think she'd be the one with the impetus or motivation. I'd sowed some seeds in her mind a few weeks back about an antiques dealer in Tetouan. An old French guy, who was a connoisseur of objet d'art that Ayoub had told me about. He had a reputation for collecting rare and exotic heirlooms from impoverished inheritors. They were for sale only through private channels, creating an exclusivity that Fiona obviously couldn't resist. Having had some time to think about it she was now keen to go and check out his inventory.

I played it coy so as not to raise any suspicion, 'I didn't think you were that keen on going up there, what with all the renovations going on in the workshop, and the Gnaoua festival coming up.'

Fiona was shaking her head as I spoke, 'No,' she answered, 'it'd be great to get away. Honestly, seeing those builders everyday is doing me in. I can phone to check up on their progress, and anyway we should definitely get that aid stuff to those poor people.'

In full plan-making mode now I went on to suggest, 'We should go just before and during Eid, then you won't have to deal with all those sad goats and sheep bleating for their lives on the rooftops. Plus the traffic will be better over the holiday.'

Fiona nodded, 'Yeah, that sounds good Kasha, and when we get back we'll have the Gnaoua to enjoy, perfect.'

Fiona slid her car keys across the table, 'Find out who we need to contact up in Ghazoua to pick up the aid donations, then use the Merc to go and get it. I'll see what I can glean from my contacts about where the aid should be dropped off in the mountains. It's going to be quite an adventure eh.'

Our eyes met, and Fiona read my puzzled look.

'Keep the Merc until your bike's fixed, let's try to get organised and leave at the end of the week. There's not much room here so keep the aid at your place till we're ready to go.'

A BOTTLE OF WHISKEY

The alcohol shop in Mogador lurks quietly on Avenue Al Massira, a busy street of small shops just outside the medina. Discreetly wedged between a mobile phone outlet and a boutique selling women's wear, the door to this shop is always open. It is so perhaps in an attempt to reassure customers, as its boarded windows and faded blue sun shade create a shadowy, illicit ambience. From the outside, the interior of the shop looks dark and foreboding. A passerby may, however, not even notice the place, missing it amongst the milling Moroccan shoppers and the many pavement displays of cheap fashion accessories.

In truth the shop is trying not to be noticed, but everyone in Mogador knows where it is. Those leaving the place will exit with their purchases wrapped in brown paper or squeezed into cardboard boxes, the stigma attached to alcohol somehow being dissipated by superficial concealment. Drinking beer, wine or spirits is Haram, but while like smoking it is tolerated, alcoholic drinks are not normally consumed in public. Those found lying incapacitated in the streets are dealt with harshly and will find themselves sobering up in the filth of the town's prison. Nevertheless, the alcohol shop is a highly profitable establishment in Mogador, frequented by many and controlled by the Bourkh family, primarily Aziz.

*****

Mustaffa wanted to celebrate. He felt good. He had 3000

dirhams in his pocket and wouldn't need to work for a month. Today he'd got up late, similarly to most days in fact. He'd slept through morning prayers with the fog of kiff addling his mind. Even the hubbub of children arriving at the village preschool next door hadn't woken him. His mother was nowhere to be seen, but had left him cold coffee in a saucepan on the stove. On the bus ride into Mogador he'd convinced himself he'd buy her something nice, like a scarf. Such laudable and good intentions were short-lived though, thoughts of his mother vanishing as his step quickened towards the alcohol shop.

He bought a bottle of whiskey, looking forward to its heady stupor, and an afternoon of lolling in the medina watching scantily-clad tourists. What else was there for him. No wife, no home. He had some olive trees to tend, and chickens to defend from snakes, but no children who wanted to know him. Mustaffa didn't mind. It was Allah's will that had brought him to this moment in his life, and Mustaffa was at peace with his destiny. It was hardly surprising though that his mother chided him for being lazy and useless. He wanted to forget everything and be happy.

Finding a shady spot within the walled gateway at Bab Doukkala, Mustaffa sat down amongst a gaggle of men selling SIM cards and socks. He opened the whiskey and took a furtive drink. The cooler air under the medina gateway was refreshing, and the crush of pedestrians, with their colour and chatter made Mustaffa feel like he had some company.

In front of him an awkwardly large vegetable barrow, filled with fresh carrots and tomatoes, brought the traffic flow to a halt. Jammed up hard against it was a motorcyclist, the huge pannier of warm baguettes strapped to his bike's rear seat completely filling the available road space. With the air heating in the passageway, and people squeezed against its stone walls, a general sense of alarm rippled through the crowd. Three cats scuttled from amongst the legs of those who were trapped. A child called out for its mother. Two big chickens, being held by their legs, became a hysterical flurry of feathers, the motor cyclist revved his engine and the breathable air filled with fumes. There followed a brief panic, some pushing, raised voices and eventually the motorcycle was dragged backwards, letting the traffic flow again.

This was all a bit too chaotic for what Mustaffa had in mind. He'd managed to have a surreptitious drink in the middle of the melee but this was not what he had imagined when he set out earlier to celebrate. Tucking the bottle of whiskey, now only two thirds full, into a pocket in his jacket he made off through the dark, salt-stained medina passages of the mellah. Here the air was almost wet, it being close to the sea wall and obscured from sunlight by the mish-mash and congestion of buildings.

By the time he got to his friend Solieman's shop Mustaffa was feeling and looking a bit worse for wear. He hadn't noticed until he'd stepped in some sheep offal, all slippery and bloody, that he'd left his shoes behind with the men at Bab Doukkala. Subsequently, and after wiping his feet mostly clean, he had bought some cheap flip flops to tide him over and, on what he convinced himself was a whim, bought some silver Tuareg jewellery and a Bedouin teapot.

Sadly, and in reality, his purchases had been both a misjudged, and whiskey fuelled, attempt to woo two Spanish tourists who'd caught his eye. His efforts were all in vain when the women had diverted their eyes away from his friendly but toothless smile towards the smell of his feet. He'd tried to nonchalantly hide his flip flops under a small table displaying wooden camel-shaped fridge magnets. It was too late, the two women had turned their backs on him, and he could feel a cat licking his toes. Shaking Solieman's hand at the threshold of his shop, Mustaffa handed him the teapot.

'Good day my brother,' Solieman said with a welcoming smile, 'what can I do for you this afternoon?'

'Can I see the menu, you have something special today?' Mustaffa replied, with a bit of a slur in his voice.

'We have the usual, of course, the best in Mogador, but for a little extra today there is a new face, a belly dancer from Marrakech, you want to see her?'

Mustaffa smiled, wobbled a bit and got out some crumpled bank notes from his pocket. Solieman took the money, stepped aside, and pointed to the shadows behind him, 'Follow him,' he directed Mustaffa, pointing to a burly looking thug who shuffled out of the dimness and grunted at Mustaffa.

TANGIER

'That's the Spanish mainland you can see,' the well-dressed Abdul Hacke informed Ayoub from behind his shoulder.

Ayoub was standing in the alcove of a large, high ceilinged room. The french windows to the balcony in front of him were open, a sea breeze was blowing gently and the Tangier skyline stretched out before him.

'The Portuguese named this road, Rua Gibraltar,' Abdul continued, leaning forward and gesturing with his hand out across the city. 'Look at all those balconies with their arcades and fancy iron work. The colonialists may have left their mark but now we have control, we have the power. This is our North African fortress, our king's summer home, our medina and harbour. There is no other place like this in the whole of Morocco my brother.' And with an endearing squeeze of Ayoub's neck, Abdul finished by saying, 'We have the keys to the Mediterranean, and we play by our own rules.'

Ayoub turned away from the view, and made his way back across the room to the sofa and chairs where they'd been sitting.

*****

Hussain had driven Ayoub from the commercial port, to Majir in the heart of Tangier. They'd parked outside an ornate european-styled apartment block, with expensive upmarket shops nestled in its ground floor, and an arched entrance way. Midway up one of Tangier's many hills, its balconies afforded a vista across the city to the maze of rooftops in the medina, and beyond to the harbour.

There, in a spacious third floor residence he'd been introduced to Abdul and his brother, Siad. The four of them had eaten supper in the company of another man, who'd sat silently in the corner of the room. They had eaten dates, a bean stew with beef and discussed football, cars, women and eventually business.

'So you met Hussain in prison, in Beni-Abbes?' Siad had asked Ayoub.

'Yeah, there were six of us Moroccans together in one room, we had a lot of time to talk, I guess we were there for three months,' Ayoub replied, looking at Hussain who nodded in confirmation.

'I know why Hussain had gone to Algeria, but you weren't there to collect pills, what was your plan?'

Ayoub studied Siad. He was wearing an expensive white shirt open at the neck, and a pair of loose suit trousers. He was well groomed, wore a stylish watch and was missing, if Ayoub wasn't mistaken, half of his right index finger. This was a man whose wealth had obviously come at a some cost to himself. A man who had means and a mean streak. A man who sent his cousin to collect pills, thousands of doses of ice, from a country crawling with far more secret police and informers than Morocco. This was a man who was not obliged to care much about his cousin, and would feel absolutely no duty towards Ayoub.

'I was looking for opportunities,' Ayoub responded. 'After Covid my town, Mogador, was empty, I had to do something, find a future. I made the journey to Algeria hoping there would be something I could bring back. It didn't work out though.'

Now it was Siad's turn to study Ayoub, 'I hope your plan for this merchandise that you want to buy from the Rif works out better than this trip to Algeria. You'll get a lot longer in jail if you're caught moving stuff out of the Rif mountains, that's if you're lucky.'

Ayoub rubbed his chin, reached down into his backpack, pulled out the manila folder containing Mustaffa's seafaring documents, and put it on the table. Tapping his index finger on the cover, he looked at Siad, 'Everything is organised to ship the merchandise down the coast, we just need a go-between to deal with the farmers in the Rif.'

'And you think we can help?' Siad asked.

'I got the impression from Hussain that this was the sort of thing you might be able to help us with, yes?' Ayoub replied.

At this point Abdul sat forward in his chair and looked intently at Ayoub, 'Well my brother, since you are family, we will help. This is a bad business that you are choosing. It's not a business for amateurs.'

Ayoub swallowed.

'If you want to pay us we can bring the merchandise down from the Rif to the port. No problems. The farmers and the police will all be dealt with, but this will cost you.' Abdul paused.

Ayoub knew this was probably the safest and easiest course of action.

Abdul continued, 'If you want to make your own arrangements with the farmers, fine. Hussain can help you with this. I'll make sure that our other business associates do not get in your way.'

'Yeah you don't want to have to deal with the other traffickers. They'll definitely steal whatever you've got, and maybe cut your throat for being there,' Siad interjected.

'What do you want in return?' Ayoub asked.

'If you deal with the farmers, move what you have bought

down to the port on your own, all we'll want is 1%. Not in cash, but from the product. This is the best choice for us. A warning my brother, this is dangerous for you.'

*****

Ayoub knew in his bones that this was not a good arrangement. Negotiating with the farmers wouldn't be too tricky but transporting the merchandise from the mountains to the port at Tangier, that was going to be difficult, and dangerous. Why would he agree to such a plan? They'd probably have to get through at least five police checkpoints, where there'd be sniffer dogs, and perhaps other things that they didn't know about. Could they really trust Abdul and his brother, and who was the man in the corner listening to everything? Ayoub wanted the money though, he would rather die trying to get rich, than live a life being poor. Abdul's favoured option had its appeal, after all it would cost less, and they wouldn't have to have anything more to do with these dodgy traffickers. So Ayoub ignored the warning, made arrangements with his new associates, and went to pray.

THE RADAR STATION

From a distance the three figures on the beach were difficult to make out. Raising my hand to shield my eyes from the sun's morning glare, I could just see the blurry shapes of a donkey and a dog, standing near to a fisherman working in the shallow surf. The sky was clear blue, the wind was blowing from the north and I was sitting beneath two tall mobile phone masts on the hilly ridge overlooking the ocean. The coastline stretched out empty and barren to the north, and to the south it was possible to just make out the hazy outline of Hilal and then Mogador beyond.

I could have met Ayoub at his home in Mogador, but knowing how pervasive gossip and rumour were in these parts I wanted to avoid any link between myself and Ayoub in the minds of the town. I'd set out on foot at dawn and followed the winding track that was barely suitable for motor vehicles, through the short gnarly tamarisk trees that lined the hills, to the clearing where the masts stood. Two kilometres beneath me lay the concrete shape of the single storey radar station, its rotating antenna and flat white walls distinctly setting it aside from the arid flora and sand dunes.

The radar station had been built 20 years ago, following 9/11, as a programme of civil defence and was part of a network of similar outposts located at 10 km intervals all the way down the coast. The stations had an overlapping range of 200 nautical miles, providing the military and scientific teams that staffed them with an overview of maritime traffic, and climatic conditions. Each station had a crew of three gendarmes and two scientists working on a rotation of two day shifts, uploading scheduled reports twice a day and maintaining a vigilant eye on the beach. At night time two of the crew would sleep in a lean-to that had been constructed from a wooden frame and tarpaulin, beside the main building on the beach. It's one open end gave the occupants unobstructed access to sounds and activity on the beach after dark.

I watched a figure emerge onto the roof of the station, stand by the guard rail surveying the horizon and then disappear. Moments later the same figure reappeared at ground level, left the radar station and made his way across the beach towards the fisherman and his animal companions. This man would not be able to hear the vehicle that was driving up the track towards the masts where I was sitting. I hoped that the men on the beach wouldn't pay any heed to the dust cloud that it was kicking up.

THE TRUTH

Ayoub parked the Merc in the clearing, turned the ignition off and put his head in his hands. He was tired. I opened the driver's door, greeted him, drew a deep breath through my nose and said, 'What's that smell?'

'It's Mustaffa, he's asleep in the back,' Ayoub answered, swivelling in his seat and climbing out of the vehicle. 'Here, you can have these keys back,' he said, offering me the Mercedes fob that still had my motorcycle keys attached to it. 'You're not going to get much sense out of Mustaffa for a while. Nor me probably. I picked him up from the medina police station in the early hours. They'd found his phone and called me. He's been asleep in the back of the Merc ever since. Stinks of whiskey. Keeps mumbling something about Ingrid being a bad one. A zigzag.'

I sighed, this wasn't what I had been expecting.

Ayoub carried on, 'I think something happened at Solieman's place yesterday evening, Mustaffa got a bit leery I guess. They called the gendarmes. Apparently Ingrid was working at Solieman's, reckon things got a bit rowdy. You know how Mustaffa can get.' I nodded, and we both leaned against the Merc's warm bonnet, neither of us saying anything for a moment. Then, thoughtfully, I asked, 'You don't think Ingrid would double cross us do you? Mustaffa knows all about our schedule and delivery plan. If she could get that to Bourkh he'd be able to ambush us on the beach, that would be that.'

Ayoub remained quiet and then asked, 'If he'd told her anything he wouldn't have been kicked out of Solieman's though would he?.......By the way it cost 400 dirham to get him released.

Did you get the rest of the cash for expenses from Otto?'

'Yeah. Yeah, I got the cash from Ingrid while you were away in Tangier. We're covered for the farmers, our expenses and the traffickers. This 400 dirham is not a problem,....but maybe Mustaffa is. What do you think? Perhaps we should find someone else. A villager who won't get drunk and arrested as soon as they have a bit of money in their pocket.' I let out an exasperated breath, 'guess it's too late now.'

Ayoub was nodding and grinned, 'I'll have the 400 back, that was out of my own pocket. We won't need any money for the traffickers though, I'll tell you about that in a bit. Hussain's ready to set the deal up with the Rif farmers at the end of the week.....you got things covered so we can get up to Tetouan for then?'

'Yeah,' I answered, 'we're going to drive up there on Friday. Fiona and I are taking the Merc, we're visiting that French antique dealer you told me about. The plan's for you to drive a pick-up full of donated aid from the expats in Ghazoua. Ingrid may have tried to double cross us, but she did get her French and German chums to stump up the cash to hire a pick-up.'

Ayoub and I both felt the Merc shift on its axles slightly. 'He's waking up,' Ayoub said, catching a reflection of himself in my sunglasses, as he turned to look over his shoulder.

I shuffled around to the side of the vehicle to get a look through the door window. Mustaffa was still asleep, lying like a rag on the reed matting that lined the rear cargo space of the Merc. 'No, he's still snoring away,' I informed Ayoub, opening the driver's side door, 'we should take him home, maybe we'll get the truth out of him by the time we get to his mother's.'

'The truth,' Ayoub repeated, as he opened the passenger door and got in beside me. 'Whatever Mustaffa tells us will be the truth, no Moroccan ever speaks anything but the truth, Kasha.' Ayoub sounded like an imam giving a sermon. He carried on,

'Even if everyone knows that what is being said is a lie, that is forgotten and it becomes the truth. You'll find it's the same for every working Moroccan. They don't think about the future, about judgement, about the fiery pit of Jahannam.'

'You reckon?' I responded.

'Of course, Moroccans live from day to day. Some of their choices are not good, but they keep their own conscience. They do salat, Ramadan, sacrifices at Eid. They are not thinking of tomorrow, or the record of their wrongs.'

I was listening and turned the key in the ignition. The engine purred, and the wheels shifted in the soft sand beneath the vehicle. Mustaffa let out a groan of discomfort and I recalled what Ayoub had once told me about being a good muslim. In a world where there is lots of temptation he'd said there are only a few pious muslims who refrain from Haram.These souls will have a very short inquisition when arriving at Jahannam, oddly similar to those of beggars who have been too poor to indulge in forbidden pleasures.The words that come from these Moroccans' mouths can be trusted, for they do speak the truth, they can afford to speak the truth. Their lives are either worthy enough, or so modest, that they have no need for dishonesty.

As I mulled this over Ayoub finished saying what he'd started, 'Mustaffa will tell us the truth about Ingrid, and any deal he suspects she is devising with Aziz Bourkh behind our backs. Whether we believe him or not, may have consequences for us. What is for certain is that Allah will know if he is telling the truth. This will have consequences for him when his toes touch the burning flames of Jahannam.'

I raised my eyes from the sandy track that we were following back to the main coastal road, catching Ayoub's intense brown-eyed gaze. I smiled at him, flipped the indicator, and with a brief spin of the rear wheels set off in the direction of Barnook.

'The real question though, Kaska, is why are you involved in this scheme? Mustaffa and I will both benefit from the money, we need the money to build our lives, but this isn't really the case for you my brother. We have simple, uncomplicated motives for doing business with Aziz and the traffickers, and it is my hope that Allah will understand and accept the penance I make each day. You though, you don't need the money, and you are definitely not seeking any atonement. I don't understand why you are risking so much, for benefits I cannot see you need.'

Mustaffa was shuffling a bit in the back of the Merc, perhaps sobering up and beginning to feel the toxic cloak of his hangover.

'Can you still smell Mustaffa?' I asked Ayoub, as I glanced in the rear view mirror.

'No, not even with my big nose,' he answered, smiling.

'You know why this is?' I continued, pursuing the point, 'he still stinks, and the car is full of his stench. So why can you no longer smell him?'

Ayoub shook his head, unsure what I was getting at, and certainly not making a link between the question he'd asked me, and Mustaffa's present state of personal hygiene.

'You, my dear brother, you are a believer aren't you. You find truth and meaning in the Quran and Allah.'

'I try to be the best Muslim I can,' Ayoub replied.

'So you have a guide, a path to riches for your soul and the possibility of infinite pleasure and happiness in al-Akhirah, the afterlife.'

'Yes Kasha, but what are you getting at?'

'You know I don't see the world like this. For me there is no guide,' I replied.

Ayoub swivelled in his seat and watched me. The road

before us was slinking up into the hills that formed a craggy ridge overlooking the ocean, and would then veer inland towards the village where Mustaffa lived with his mother.

'You cannot smell Mustaffa because your nose has become used to his stink. That strong, vivid stench that made your stomach spin when you first smelt Mustaffa, it's gone now. Faded. Now, even though his smell is still sickly, you cannot even discern a whiff of him. For me, choices between good and bad are like this. Bad decisions become good ones, they fade into each other if you do them enough.

'This is how I see living, my brother. We live a life of sensation. We feel, we touch, we hear, we see. We know life through what we sense, and slowly these sensations lose their potency. We get used to them, just like you and I have got used to Mustaffa stinking of whiskey. And what do we do as the sensations around us become jaded and thin with repetition?'

I took a second to stop watching the empty country road in front of me, and looked at Ayoub.

'Maybe this is when you die?' Ayoub ventured.

'I'm not ready for that. I think we can do one of two things, brother. We can accept the creeping dullness of our living days or we can search for adventure. Seek new sensations and new experiences. The choice isn't between good and bad, but between energy and numbness. I don't have a guide like you, but I have desire and passion that I need to feed.'

This was not the response that Ayoub had expected from me. It did explain though why I was willing to risk so much without the obvious need of a financial incentive. Ayoub had to resign himself to the reality that my mind did not work like those of his fellow Moroccans.

TALES FROM MOGADOR: KASHA AND THE KIFF

ANKLES

A scorpion stirred sleepily from its shadowy lair amongst the parched dust and stones of an old dry river bed. Its sting lay limp in the early moments of the sunrise, and above it Fiona's Mercedes rattled over the narrow iron bridge that carries the main road from Mogador to Marrakech. Years ago a wide, cool river had flowed in torrents beneath this bridge, donkeys and goats would have drunk from it, and peasant farmers had used the water to irrigate their land. Now the river is gone. Beneath the bridge there just is a scorched chasm and a trickle of water from the distant Higher Atlas mountains where its source is dammed.

*****

To drive from Mogador up to the northern city of Tetouan in the highlands of the Rif is a long, two day journey that starts with a hot and taxing 170 km drive east, across the desert plateau towards Marrakech. From the city limits of Marrakech it is possible to join the auto-route system, completed in the mid 2000's, and within the speed limit of 100 kmh make almost uninterrupted progress to the mediaeval and influential north eastern city of Fez. The auto-routes are not busy, and provide a considerably quicker, and perhaps safer, path to Fez and the Atlas mountain range than the crumbling and windy country roads used by those who cannot afford, or do not wish to pay, the tolls. Either journey will encounter any number of police checkpoints, where the documents and contents of a vehicle will be scrutinised, and potentially a tax, fine or payment will be required depending on the mood of the gendarmes. From the passenger seat of the Merc I watched a pair of falcons swoop down towards the river bed, twisting in my seat to follow them as they hunted. Driving beside me, Fiona accelerated up the incline towards the Ghazoua urban area where the Hilux pickup full of aid was waiting to be collected. In the back seat Ayoub rubbed his drowsy eyes, 'this Hilux, it's fully loaded up isn't it? It'll never keep up with you two in this,' Ayoub said, opening his arms to the plush interior of the Mercedes.

'Yes, that's true,' I replied. 'I'll message you the hotel information in Fez when we get to Ingrid's, that way you'll know where to meet us if we do get separated. She's got the documents and keys for the pick-up. You'll need some cash for the tolls too. You're good for this, yeah?'

Ayoub didn't reply. The new and huge mosque being built on the outskirts of Ghazoua had caught his attention. Its concrete dome unpainted and a dull grey, was set against a landscape and sky of evocative, brilliant colour. He couldn't help thinking that the partially complete building was an apt reminder of humanity's imperfection and Allah's inscrutable presence. He was glad he'd risen early and done his morning prayer; he knew that he'd need all the benefits of his faith over the next week.

'Why's she sitting in the passenger seat?' Ayoub asked, leaning forward between Fiona and myself, as we pulled up at the rendezvous point by a small collection of kiosks and shops in central Ghazoua. Ingrid's silhouette could clearly be made out through the rear window of the pickup, as could the outline of a travel bag beside her. I got out, and while Ayoub collected his array of belongings from the back seat, I made my way to the Hilux as Ingrid ran her window down.

'I need a lift to Marrakech,' she said, without pausing for introductions.

I looked at the German woman through the open door

window. Her piercing blue eyes, smooth skin and thin shapely lips hypnotising me for a moment. 'That's nice. I am well thanks, so is Ayoub and Fiona. I'm guessing that this is a bit of an unplanned trip,' I replied, regaining a bit of composure by allowing my eyes to stray from her intense gaze to the sacks and boxes stacked in the pickup's bed.

'You're going that way aren't you?' Ingrid continued, ignoring my niceties. 'I've got some work in Marrakech this evening. I'll need to let them know if I'm coming and get someone to feed my animals. Do you think one of you could drop me in Marrakech?'

Putting my hands in my trouser pockets, I smiled and said, 'I should think we can sort something out for you Ingrid. Ayoub was meant to be driving with us, to Rabat and then over to Fez on the auto-routes, but I'm sure he can make a detour to Marrakech, for you. Let me talk to him.'

'Thank you, Kasha.' Ingrid responded, a glint of success in her eye. 'Tell him I'll make it worth his while,' she added, watching Ayoub clamber out of the Merc as I began to explain the slight change in arrangements to him.

'Yeah, that's fine brother, I'll take her into the city, and then catch you up in Fez later,' Ayoub had said, and then as he made his way towards the Hilux he asked, 'By the way does Fiona know anything about what we're up to, have you told her?'

I shook my head.

*****

The land between Mogador, on the north western coast of Africa, and the Atlas mountain range that towers over Marrakech is a dry, barren and sparsely populated plateau. Mostly un-irrigated, the terrain is bare, stoney, and sparsely covered with hardy fruit-bearing shrubs and vegetation, providing just enough to support small scale farms and animal herders. The cross country mercantile traffic, requiring fuel, accommodation and refreshments, sustains several minor towns between Mogador and Marrakech. All of these settlements are sun drenched, have a shabby, fatigued flavour, and eke out an existence in the emptiness that stretches from the mountains to the ocean. Travelling east in the early morning Ayoub and Ingrid could both feel the warmth of the sun. 'Is there somewhere to charge my phone, do you think?' Ingrid queried, fiddling with her phone and charger cable.

Ayoub glanced down across at the dashboard and pointed to the stereo where there was a charging point, 'If you keep it off while it's plugged in, it'll charge faster,' he volunteered.

'That'd be good,' Ingrid said, grinning back at him. 'I've got people to tell what I'm up to, and my cats will need feeding later. The battery's completely flat, how long do you think it'll take?'

'Not long.'

'Thanks,' Ingrid responded, tucking the phone into the console between the pair of them, and then stretching her legs. She'd got dressed quickly this morning, throwing on a loose cotton blouse and a double layer wrap-round silk sarong. Easing back into the passenger seat she slid off her sandals, put her feet up against the windscreen and closed her eyes.

'Here, put this 'casha' under your feet.' Ayoub suggested, handing her a small woollen blanket he'd brought with him. 'You get some rest if you like, it'll take us an hour or two before we reach Marrakech.'

'You're kind, wake me if you need me.'

Ayoub had spent little time in the company of foreign women, and certainly hadn't had the chance to be so close to a sleeping beauty like Ingrid. At 32 he was still unmarried, and like all Moroccan men obliged, and frustrated, by the principles of his faith and the modesty required by Halal dating. It wasn't long before he could tell that Ingrid had drifted off, her sarong had slipped down her calves revealing the slender bones of her ankles and the soft hairless skin of her legs. She stirred dreamily, as the road meandered its way towards the mountainous peaks on the horizon.

How different this was from the experience he had had several months ago, when a young village woman he'd been allowed to speak with in the company of a chaperone, had briefly removed her hijab and shown him her hair. At the time this had been a charged and fleeting moment of intimacy, now he had an abundance of the feminine form upon which his eyes could feast and for which his soul would not suffer. Beneath him the engine hummed, the faraway snowy peaks beyond Marrakech shone and his mind began to wander.

HELP ME!

Ayoub heard something. A shout, a cry, a voice he knew. His eyes were closed. He could feel his skin against the soft woollen blanket and the hard earth beneath him. There was that noise again. He breathed in, and listened. A shiver ran across his shoulders; he remembered being warm, now there was a breeze. His back was bare, his body clammy with drying sweat. He let his breath out slowly, still listening and opened his eyes.

Beneath his head was his shirt, and almost at the end of his nose was the black rear tyre of the Hilux. His eyes widened and focused on the empty arid ground that he could see through the space under the vehicle. It was chilly in the shadow cast by the Hilux. He didn't have his trousers on, and reached backwards to grab the blanket's edge to pull it over his shoulder.

He stopped. That was definitely his name he could hear. Sitting up, he took a short breath, his heart quickened and memories of the morning flashed through his giddy head. A wave of nausea, or was it guilt, washed through his body. He knew he wasn't thinking straight, the kiff that he'd shared with Ingrid was still rich and pervasive in his blood.

To his right he heard a scream. It was Ingrid's voice, clear, shrill and terrified. Why wasn't she beside him? Where was she? What was happening? Ayoub opened his mouth, but nothing came out.

Standing up, he clumsily snatched his trousers from where they'd been discarded, and scanned the flat, sparsely wooded space from where he'd heard the calls. He wobbled, alert to the panic that he'd heard in her voice, and put a hand to his head to shield his eyes. Beyond the short stubby tamarisk trees in the foreground there was a rolling sandy landscape, shaped only by the wind and the wild creatures who'd made it their home.

He heard Ingrid again, this time there was alarm and fear in her call. Ayoub's gaze skimmed across the dusty surroundings, from clumps of shrubs and cactus to a patch of giant aloe-vera plants beside which he could just make out the shape of two baby camels and their mother. For a moment he relaxed, and felt his inner strength drain like it had in those heated, sensual exchanges on the blanket earlier. Ingrid had obviously woken up and wandered off to see the two untethered baby camels and their mother. Somehow it all didn't make sense though. If she wanted some company, why was she shrieking in a frenzy?

Ayoub found his flip-flops, and strode out across the grit and earth towards the camels. They were probably 40 metres from the secluded spot where he'd parked the Hilux, and looked as if they were grazing. He was a town boy, unfamiliar with gnarly tree roots and stoney crevices where vipers might lie, and so his progress was careful until once again he heard Ingrid's anguished cries for help.

Picking up his stride with energy and urgency he peered into the hot haze. There, in an open sandy clearing, not far from the camels, he caught sight of Ingrid in her white blouse, unnaturally low to the ground waving her arms above her head. He stopped, called out to her and then rushed forward sensing that something was wrong. Very wrong!

The nearer he got the less the scene seemed to make sense. She was shouting something repeatedly. The same word over and over. He couldn't hear anything but noise and fear, and then the word, stop, stop, stop forced its way into his head, and he stopped at the edge of the clearing.

He could only see half of Ingrid's body. She was about three metres from him. Tears were running down her face, her blouse was smudged with sandy goo and her hair tousled in thick strands. 'I'm sinking, I'm going to die Ayoub. Help me!!'

'Try and spread your weight out,' Ayoub replied, 'open your legs as wide as they will go, and don't wiggle.'

'I can't move my legs, they're stuck and it's sucking me down, help me, help me Ayoub,' Ingrid pleaded!

'I'm going to get some rope. I'll be back, it'll be okay,' Ayoub said, trying to sound reassuring as he turned to sprint as fast as he could back to the Hilux.

Behind him she was still calling and shouting as though she was being left to disappear into the earth alone. Passing through the glade of tamarisk trees one of his flip-flops slid from his foot, and he winced with pain as he stubbed his toes against stones and debris lying beneath the trees. She was still shouting, screaming in fact, as he arrived back in a flurry at the Hilux. Both ends of the rope that had been used to secure the sacks onto the bed of the pick-up were tied with thick complicated knots. The rope itself was dry and frayed, and not easy to twist and pull. Ayoub teased one of the securing knots with his fingers and then his teeth, yanking it hard when it seemed that it wouldn't come loose.

Ingrid felt helpless. She could sense the cold, deathly grip of the earth dragging her down. Her legs, hips and torso were immovable and seemed set in stone. What a dreadful way to die she thought as she spread her arms across the surface of the quicksand, in one last effort to keep her neck and head from the breathless tomb of the land.

She was quiet now, saving what energy she had for the last minutes of her life. Ayoub sensed the silence and hoped he wasn't too late, pushing and probing at the knot until finally it gave in, and came loose. Then, almost in a choreographed motion, he pulled the rope all the way through the clips, clutched two sacks full of clothing under each of his arms and made off back towards Ingrid.

The camels had gone; Ayoub couldn't see Ingrid's arms although with the rope and sacks all about him it was difficult to see anything much. By the time he got to the edge of the clearing she'd gone. Her head had disappeared, just her right arm above the elbow remained visible over the surface of the sand.

It took seconds for him to loop the rope around a tree stump near the edge of the clearing, tie the other end around his waist and then throw the sacks out over the quicksand. Clambering onto and then lying down over the sacks, the sand rippled under Ayoub's weight, distracting him slightly as Ingrid's hand finally slipped from view and into the earth.

Shuffling up as near as he dared, Ayoub thrust his arm into the sand, pushing it deep and stretching out his fingers to find her. There was nothing. He tried again, shifting a bit on the sacks, and plunging his arm into the sand, at a different angle.

This time he touched her. Her thin fingers clasping, clinging and seizing hold of his. Working his way down to her slender wrist he gripped it with all his might and dragged her upwards. He could feel her pulse, her will to live, her desire to breathe, and when he finally lay exhausted with her at the edge of the clearing, he thought that perhaps he understood a little of what Kasha had meant by the potency of life.

RED FLAGS

The autoroute system that links the major Moroccan cities and urban conurbations looks new, and is as yet unruined. Mostly constructed with a concrete bitumen surface, the grey and relatively empty network carries traffic with a bouncy hum from Tangier, south via Rabat and Casablanca to Agadir, and east to Fez. The customary neglect and overuse that typically befalls almost every commodity and facility in the country has for the time being been avoided by the 2000km of twin lane toll roads. This is mainly because these cross country arteries have to be paid for with cash, and thus it is only the wealthier commercial enterprises and affluent Moroccans who can afford the comfort and ease that the autoroutes offer.

'He's going to give her a lift to Marrakech,' I told Fiona as I clambered back onto the passenger seat of the Merc. 'It's probably better anyway for him to travel with the Hilux and all those sacks along the country roads to Fez,' I continued, as Fiona turned the ignition, and pulled away from the shops in Ghazoua, giving me a puzzled look. 'I mean that pick-up would stand out on the autoroutes like a european wearing a djellaba. The police would take one look at it, pull him over at the toll booths and insist he unpacks every single parcel. They'd crawl all over it. Maybe insist the sacks are emptied so their dogs can riffle through the stuff. After all that, they'll leave him to repack it. I can just imagine his Moroccan temperament unravelling and his buttons being pushed. It'd cost him backsheesh too. He's much better off taking it steady along the country roads. It might be slower but he's more likely to keep clear of the inquisitive gendarmes and have a comfortable journey.'

'Mmm...' Fiona replied absentmindedly, seeming slightly uninterested in what I had to say. 'He's going to meet us at the hotel in Fez, yeah?' she eventually remarked, the landscape of the Moroccan interior opening up in front of us, and the outline of the Higher Atlas mountain range cutting a craggy line on the horizon.

An hour or two later, with the air conditioning in the Merc now turned up fully and Fiona's playlist of Gnaoua music set to repeat, we finally saw the entryway to the N1, and our route north.

'What's with all these national flags, do you think?' Fiona asked, peeling off the Marrakech road and following a flag lined slip road towards a row of gleaming toll booths, and a queue of traffic.

'They look great don't they, I love the green pentacle on that deep red!' I replied. 'Did you not notice them in Mogador?'

'I thought they were for the tourists,' Fiona remarked, joining the line of waiting vehicles, 'but they're everywhere, what's that about?'

I drew a breath, 'They call it the King's Day. The flags are a reminder of the king's accession to the throne from his father. They're red to show his bloodline to Fatima, Mohamed's daughter, and some say that the pentacle is a reference to Soloman's seal.'

The Merc was stationary and Fiona looked blankly at me. 'Soloman's a prophet,' I said, looking at her.

'I know that,' she responded abruptly, adding, 'the prophets are all men in Islam.'

'I'm pretty sure that's not the case,' I responded, 'and actually I would have thought that you'd have liked Soloman. He had a reputation for bringing unity to his people, and reportedly could do magic and speak to animals.'

'I love animals Kasha, you know that, but you and I really differ over this male domination thing. Without mother earth we're nothing, the Gaia spirit of life is female, it predates everything. All the Abrahamic religions and science, Solomon included, they all owe their energy to the goddess.' Fiona paused, and then slipping the clutch, let the Merc creep forward in the queue, 'Look at all these red flags, perched on the end of long straight sticks. That's the male ego all over. Excited and wanting attention, but not really knowing what to do with itself.'

I sat quietly, music and cool air filled the Merc, and while we edged our way patiently towards the toll booth Fiona finished her tirade.

'I like men, Kasha,' she said, 'I just don't think they should be in charge. There's a reason why all the beautiful women in this country are kept at home, or wrapped up in hijab if they go out. The men are terrified and so weak that unless they practically imprison the women they cannot be at peace. In this country a woman's reputation, her whole future, can be completely derailed by an indiscreet show of affection or caress in public. The sorts of everyday interactions that Europeans might take for granted are totally off limits here. You know, in public there's absolutely no touching between men and women, and any behaviour to the contrary will be a social curse on that woman. What sort of world, what sort of life for women, is that, Kasha?'

I didn't have time to answer, for as we emerged from the toll booth a gendarme with gold rimmed glasses and a holstered handgun, beckoned us over to the police checkpoint. As Fiona's window opened, and the Merc came to a rest, the gendarme leaned forward, and ignoring Fiona, asked me in French for the vehicle documents.

Fiona could smell the cologne on the gendarme, and although she knew little Arabic she was quite competent using the French she'd learnt at school. Turning to him, and noticing in her wing mirror his colleague inspecting the rear of the Merc, she asked him pointedly, 'I'm driving, why aren't you asking me for my licence and the documents?'

The gendarme's nose twitched as he turned his gaze to Fiona and looked long into her blue eyes. Twisting his head he spat on the ground, squeezed the car door handle so it swung open in his hand, and gruffly issued a command.

'Please get out of the car, madame.'

TALES FROM MOGADOR: KASHA AND THE KIFF

A TRAY OF CAKES

The monotonous drone coming from the Merc's tyres on the concrete surface of the autoroute was aptly annoying and intrusive. I had got into the driver's seat while the gendarme had searched Fiona and hadn't said anything when she'd clambered back into the vehicle with a sigh. Was she angry with the police officer, or disappointed in herself for provoking him? For a moment or two I wondered whether the humiliation of being frisked at the side of the carriageway up against the Merc, would make her reconsider her attitude or simply reinforce it.

Over the hour or so that followed I felt her stewing in the seat next to me. Even the drama of a private ambulance screaming by, its red flashing lights on and its siren screeching didn't break the spell of silence between us. We didn't exchange a word, nor a glance, and just had lilting music and road hum for company. Then, north of Casablanca, having skirted the city's commercial sprawl and being overlooked by its IKEA, DHL and other multinational outlets, Fiona announced without a smile, that she needed a break. 'Don't pull into that McDonald's though,' she said, as we drove beneath a giant M sign that loomed above the carriageway.

How out of place and incongruous such a sign would have seemed in Mogador, I thought, although perhaps the appearance of such entities here in Casablanca is merely a prelude to similar businesses eventually arriving there. I hoped not, and carried on driving until, pulling in behind a passenger coach, I flicked the right hand indicator and drove the Merc up a slip road and into a service station.

There were virtually no other vehicles in the car park, and the casual observer could easily be mistaken in thinking that the place was actually shut. There were no djellaba-wearing men with beards, standing smoking cigarettes or drinking tea at a table in the shade. No charcoal burners piping the smell of roasting sardines, or tagine, into the air. The place was tidy, there was no litter, nor stray cats and dogs lying sleepily under tables in the hope of a discarded morsel. The windows were clean, and the canopies that shielded those inside the building from the bright sunshine, weren't tousled and torn. Not that there was anyone inside, the diner and its accompanying cafe were both empty, save for a few bored staff looking at their phones.

This vision of cleanliness and order was quickly shattered though. For as soon as the coach that we had followed into the service station came to rest, a gaggle of hijab-wearing women and their children emerged from a hideaway in an adjacent piece of woodland. Keeping close to the wall of the diner they sneaked towards the stationary coach hoping to make a few hasty sales. This mischievous group was part of a larger organised gang that made a living selling cakes and drinks without a licence, up and down the autoroutes. Walking across the empty car park we caught sight of two security guards marching purposely out from the building towards the women and children, who then split up and fled.

*****

Sitting together by a window, with coffee and patisseries, Fiona at last regained something of her mojo. Nudging me with her elbow, she smiled as one of the security guards had his cap blown from his head by the wind. His indignity, and that of his colleague, was compounded by nature as together they hurriedly pursued the slightly dishevelled children into the fields beyond the service station perimeter. Once the security men were out of sight, the women returned to the scene from their hiding place behind the disused car wash, their loose kaftans and hijabs flailing in the breeze.

We continued to watch the compelling episode unfold, as the women crossed the empty car park towards the coach, tentatively raising their trays of cakes to the driver's window. There was an air of comedy to proceedings, especially when the security guards reappeared and set about shooing the women away from the coach, and in the background the children re-emerged behind them. 'There are some things you just can't stop or change,' I said, sipping my coffee. 'These security men, they're never going to stop these families trying to make a living. They can chase them as much as they like, they can be cruel and vicious. Even though they might have what they think is the moral high ground, it won't change the way things are.'

I let my words linger; Fiona continued to watch proceedings out in the car park. 'I just can't help myself wanting to change it though,' she eventually replied, taking a bite from one of the pastries. 'All this male dominance, it annoys me so much. I mean look at these guys out there, the women are running rings round them, in fact even the children are. It's all wrong, Kasha!'

Fiona had a habit of talking with her mouth full, one of the several things I couldn't learn to ignore about her. Deciding to embrace my complex, I turned to face her. 'Things are changing though, Fiona,' I said, 'look at the lives that Moroccan women can live in the towns and cities. They can go to school and university, be doctors and lawyers, unmarried couples can even live together. I know it's not like that in the countryside but change like you want, radical and comprehensive change, that will take time. You, and your Gaia, will have to be patient and even then it might not happen.'

Fiona was staring at me. She didn't look convinced.

'There are things in this country, ways of living, that are etched really deeply into the psyche of the people. Most of it is to do with their ancestors and the Quran, it defines their bodies and minds. What they believe and do. It affects everything, even everyday stuff like..... you'll never stop some Moroccans killing geckos. Even if you persuade them that geckos are harmless and useful, their beliefs about the geckos trying to harm Abraham are sown so deeply into the way they see the world that nothing will make them change.'

'That doesn't make it right.' Fiona pushed back at me. 'The whole setup's so feudal. I mean.... when are they going to catch up?'

'That's the whole point.' I replied, 'they don't want to catch up. In fact if outside forces or foreigners try to be a catalyst for change it'll only entrench their views and behaviour further. Kind of like what happened with that gendarme earlier when you pressed his buttons.'

Outside, the coach that we'd followed into the service station was reversing out of its parking bay. 'You're as annoying as them,' Fiona said, standing up, 'shall we go?'

I stood too and followed her towards the door. The diner was empty again, its clean floors and piped arabesque music making it an odd and bland imitation. I felt the hot breeze on my face as I followed Fiona through the open door and checked my phone. 'Oow, looks like Ayoub and Ingrid have had a problem,' I said, 'says he's had to go to the hospital in Marrakech. Give me a moment, I'll just call him.'

Fiona was back in the driver's seat by the time I had finished catching up with Ayoub's misadventures. 'You'll never believe what happened,' I said, glancing up to the sky, 'Ingrid's in the hospital, Ayoub's going to spend the evening in Marrakech and drive to Fez in the morning.'

THE PHONE

'**H**otel Paris' was like many other two-star city centre riads in Morocco. Built above a row of shops it had a steep staircase at its entrance, and was cheap and well worn. Ayoub had checked in last night after leaving Ingrid at the Clinique International hospital in the French quarter of Marrakech, and paid for the Hilux to be parked in a disused warehouse near to the medina. He hadn't washed this morning mostly because the toilets in the hotel were blocked and their rancid overflow had made the facilities unusable, but also because he could still vaguely smell Ingrid on his skin.

Having slept fitfully in the dirty bed, he'd woken early and was now sitting at a cafe just beyond one of the smaller medina gateways and its parapet. The street before him was in a state of waking. The upmarket boutiques, delicatessens, and souvenir shops, housed in the red stone archways that lined the road either side of him, were only just drawing up their steel shutters. Cats and dogs still slept in shadowy doorways, street cleaners swept up litter, and flocks of tiny house buntings flitted from perch to perch in search of breakfast crumbs.

In the distance the rumble of buses and commuter traffic could faintly be heard, but save for the occasional motorbike delivery of fresh bread Ayoub had a peaceful scene to survey. He sipped his coffee, thought about smoking a cigarette, and picked up his phone. He had two messages. The one from Mustaffa he read and replied to, signing off with a 'thumbs up and dollar' meme, and then he called me.

'Hoya, salam,' I said, picking up the call quickly. 'How are you, how's Ingrid?'

'Everything's good, brother. Ingrid's in a French university hospital, they're keeping her in for a day or two to monitor her, but I think she'll be fine.

'Good,' I responded.

'The Hilux has been locked up all night. I'm going to go and collect it in a minute, and then drive up to Fez with a couple of Moroccan guys from the hotel where I stayed. They need a lift, I could do with the company.'

'Yes I can imagine,' I replied. 'That was a crazy thing that happened yesterday, you saved her life! That's a big thing, bro. Sort of thing that happens once in a lifetime. Take it easy today. You're not going to get here before lunch are you? I'll wait for you but I think Fiona will head on up to Tetouan pretty soon. You know how impatient she gets. Apparently there's some famous antique market up there where people sell off their heirlooms to pay for Eid, and she's on a mission. To be honest with you it'll be a relief to get a bit of a break from her.'

'Yeah, she's a funny one,' Ayoub replied. 'She still doesn't know anything about our plans?'

'No, not the faintest clue. She's so wrapped up in her bubble, putting the world, or more accurately the politics of Morocco, to rights and spending her money, that our little scheme would never even enter her mind. No need to worry, she's just giving us a good diversionary and cover story should we need it.

'Okay, That's reassuring,' Ayoub responded, 'I'll get going soon and will call you when I'm nearing Fez. We could meet at the railway station, that'd be easy to find and I can eat there. Hussain messaged me saying that he's ready to look after us. You know, make the appropriate arrangements, once we get to Chefchaouen.'

'Hussain?' I repeated. 'That's your Tangier contact isn't it.'

'You should forget his name if you can,' Ayoub said in a cautionary tone. 'We'll meet him in Chaouen later, and then you'll need to completely disappear him from your memory for safety's sake Kasha, you understand?'

'Yup, call me when you're near, I'll be at the railway station from mid-day.'

*****

The road north from Marrakech carries traffic though endless half-complete concrete suburbs, over the dried-out river bed of the Oued Zat and past the city's palatial-looking football stadium. Stopping briefly to buy four heavy-duty blue gypsum sacks, each with a capacity of 20kg, and two giant sized tractor-wheel inner tubes, Ayoub and his two passengers had made good time clearing the city limits. They'd had to pick up some glue and a couple of small compressed-air cylinders too, but the traffic was light and so far they'd not had to stop at any of the police checkpoints.

Once out into the countryside the high craggy peaks of the Atlas Mountains to the east loomed impressively over their route, snow still lingering on the highest of their slopes. Twelve thousand feet below those chilly summits the late morning air above the road was already hot, as the bright sun baked the fertile land of the foothills they drove through. There was only just enough room in the cab of the Hilux for the three of them, and the heat was beginning to make it uncomfortable. As they readjusted themselves, and after some squirming around, one of Ayoub's passengers handed him a phone with its charger wire attached.

'Aha,' Ayoub exclaimed! remembering how Ingrid had put her phone on to charge the previous morning when they'd left

Ghazoua. Holding the steering wheel with his left hand, he reached out to take the phone with his right, and brushed his thumb across its screen. It lit up, and his eyes scanned the messages that were waiting to be opened, stopping abruptly at the one from Aziz B. He wasn't expecting to see a message from him.

Ayoub snatched a breath, this was bad news. A sick and twisted ache began turning deep down in his stomach. He tried to open the phone but it was locked. He needed to concentrate on the road but couldn't resist peering down at the phone's screen, in the shadow of the dashboard. There he could just make out the first few words of Aziz's message, 'A white Mercedes, registration.....'

THE MACADAM

Barnook's main street runs from north to south, and is lined on either side by single storey dwellings and shops with flat concrete walls and roofs. For about ¼ of a km the road is home to butchers and blacksmiths, rudimentary cafes with open fire stoves, farm machinery and tobacco outlets, and food shops. The buildings are weathered, their paint is faded or peeling. Many of the shops have goods and wares tumbling onto the street and there is the smell of dogs, cats, donkeys and dirtiness in the air. In the centre of the town you'll find a number of beaten-up but functioning parked cars, a couple of which will be vintage Mercedes and old Renaults held together with wire and paint, and a group of single-axle horse-drawn buggies.

There are two speed bumps on the road as it enters the farming town from the south, put there several years ago after a series of tragic evening time accidents hàd shocked the locals into taking action. A newly constructed hamam on the southern edge of town, provides washing facilities for the majority of the town's inhabitants, and the Africa Gas petrol station gives the town a strategic significance in the locality. Barnook's understated and worn presence makes it a perfect and unlikely holding point for contraband smuggled in from the nearby fishing port of Hilal. It is also the home of many of the fishermen, who scrape together a living through farming, or trading during the spring and autumn when the ocean is too formidable to sail.

*****

Mustaffa had caught the Lima bus to Barnook. It cost five dirham, and although it was only a 15 minute ride along the road from his mother's house, had he walked through the countryside it would have taken him all morning. He had a long day ahead, with a bus ticket for an overnight ride to Tangier in his pocket. Sitting at a plastic table in the shade of the fancifully titled 'Monaco Cafe.' he stirred sugar into a small pot of mint tea, and waited. There was a little breeze, just enough to blow dust along the street, and ruffle the fur of sleeping dogs.

Absent-mindedly he checked his phone, and reread the arrangements he'd made with Adbul Latife. He shouldn't be long, Mustaffa thought to himself, looking forward to catching up with his fisherman friend. They'd drifted apart during Mustaffa's years down in Sahrawi but now, through a twist in circumstances, fate had drawn them together.

Abdul had recently married a second wife, thinking that his first was unable to bear children. He'd half finished a home for this additional wife on the land he owned outside Barnook, when the woman's extended family, some six other Moroccans, decided to move in, and simultaneously his first wife became pregnant. This all had quite an impact on Abdul Latife, who on a couple of occasions recently had sought counsel and a bit of peace, smoking kiff with Mustaffa.

It was on one of these soirees that Mustaffa mentioned the opportunity of making some extra cash to Abdul, and the pair had begun to make plans. Abdul's fishing boat and licence at Hilal was the fulcrum of their scheming, and their meeting today would involve them agreeing the final details and payments.

The business relationship between the pair was not completely straight forward. Mustaffa knew he couldn't trust Abdul, but equally Abdul wouldn't trust Mustaffa. Their bond of mutual mistrust was only being held together by the reciprocal benefits their plan would produce.

Mustaffa heard a kitten whine at his feet, glanced down the street, and then had his attention turned to a smartly-dressed middle-aged man who'd entered the cafe. The man, well groomed in clean trousers and a shirt, removed his expensive sunglasses and sat at a table with his back to Mustaffa. This was the town's Macadam, the police's go-between and informer. The man who knew everyone's business, the likes of which stretched right across the country, keeping the rich one step ahead of the poor, and maintaining control and order. All of a sudden Mustaffa was pleased that Abdul hadn't arrived yet. It would certainly provoke comment and would not be for the best if he and Abdul were seen to be mixing.

Mustaffa did not have much time to think though, for an older, djellaba-wearing Moroccan man with a small white prayer hat approached the Macadam, and spoke to him in hushed tones. His dark craggy face was slightly bowed, his boney hands twisting together in front of him as he recounted some local intel. Once he had finished, the Macadam nodded, reached into a trouser pocket and handed the man a 100 dirham note. Dutifully respectful, the man then left the scene with his money, and the Macadam sipped at the small black coffee that had been brought to his table.

Not long after this several other males made their way, one by one, to the Macadam's table, each spending time to pass on their information, answer questions, and receive a small payment passed from hand to hand courteously. Mustaffa feigned interest in his phone, on the horses feeding from bags hung from their necks in the street, on anything and everything, except the little episodes that were happening at the Macadam's table. He was pretty sure his presence and business was of little consequence to the Macadam, although it was hard for him not to feel slightly self-conscious when as the Macadam left the cafe its owner spent a furtive moment or two whispering into the informer's ear.

The sight of Abdul Latif's van pulling up beside a nearby lorry packed with squawking chickens gave Mustaffa the impetus to pay and leave the cafe, hoping that he'd hardly been noticed and be easily forgotten. Opening Abdul's van door he decided not to mention the Macadam. The less he said, the less anyone else would know, and the less danger there would be. All Abdul Latif needed to know was when the 'Mama Wats' would sail by Hilal, on her route from Tangier to Agadir, so he could be ready with his boat to help. Nothing more.

QUESTIONS, QUESTIONS.....

Fiona had driven out of Fez just after dawn, having been woken early by the call to prayer, its tones and incantations echoing throughout the maze of alleys and passageways, weaving across the fabric of the mediaeval medina, and stirring her from a restless sleep. The journey north from Mogador to Tetouan had somehow got under Fiona's skin, her unease gathering more and more momentum as the journey unfolded. Her departure now, alone, seemed apt.

The previous evening she and I had checked into the comfort of a nicely upmarket fondouk. From there we'd wandered downhill into the depths of the medina to find a restaurant away from the tourist haunts, and returned to sleep separately. It had not been a warm night, the skies overhead had been clear and starry. This should have been a visit full of awe and wonder for Fiona, but the ancient fortified city, home of former Arab sultans and Berber rulers from bygone centuries, had not cast its spell upon her. Instead it had reinforced her misgivings.

This had become doubly so when after supper we'd both surreptitiously watched two young men from our rooftop terrace, show each other their flick knives. Thinking they were safely out of sight the two european-styled Morrocans practised their moves, flashing the blades of their weapons with a discernible click and sense of menace. This incident, along with some Freudian reflections about the enormous tower they'd driven past outside Rabat simply added to her brooding.

She'd left after a small breakfast, walking out of the vehicle-less medina to collect the Merc and telling me that Ayoub and I should contact her when we eventually got to Tetouan in the next day or two. This was not quite how I'd envisaged the trip, however Fiona's departure was convenient and meant that Ayoub and I could meet up with Hussain and travel into the Rif without any complicated explanations.

*****

The palm trees that line the concourse in front of the arched facade of Fez's railway station cast shadows over a series of white marble benches. These were minimal in design, like the station building itself, creating a beautifully pure and yet simple atmosphere, and one which I was finding soothing as I waited for Ayoub. This was not as easy as it sounds, for my presence by the station was attracting the attention of mobile snack-sellers and coffee-makers, and even an old man who wanted to polish my shoes. I didn't need anything that was being offered but somehow I felt mean for saying 'maybe later' to each of them.

I knew that Mustaffa was on his way to Tangier, and that Hussain, who I'd never met but was our go-between with the farmers from the Rif, was already in Chaouen. The plan was falling into place; even Fiona's bad mood had turned out to be fortuitous. I amused myself with the idea that perhaps the angels of Ayoub's faith were aligning themselves to help us, and just as I did, I saw the Hilux pull through the traffic lights in front of the station.

Ayoub looked like a man who'd had a lot to think about. He'd dropped his passengers from Marrakech in the southern mellah district of Fez, spent the money he'd got from their fares on some cigarettes and had resisted the temptation of looking at Ingrid's phone again. He'd always been a bit resistant to getting involved in this adventure, and as soon as I hopped into the cab beside him I could tell he needed some reassurance. Before, however, I could even say more than 'hello.' all his frustration and anxiety poured out. 'Put your seatbelt on, knowing my luck at the moment we'll get pulled over for something like that today,' he snapped at me.

'You okay?' I ventured, clicking the belt together around my waist.

'Yeah, I'm okay. I mean if it's normal to save someone from suffocating in quicksand, take them to hospital and then find out that they're double-crossing you with a load of crooks who'll slit your neck for fun. Then yeah, everything is fine. How about you brother, you've been having a good time with your best friend?'

The smile on his face when he finished his little outburst was of some comfort, and yet hanging over all the things he'd been through was the reappearance of this idea that we were being double-crossed.

'What do you mean, double-crossed? I asked, as Ayoub pulled into the busy traffic flow bound for the outskirts of the city and the mountain roads. 'You're not talking about Mustaffa again are you? There's no way he's going to try and get in with the Mogador gangs, they'll eat him up and he knows that.'

Ayoub had his hands full, navigating the Hilux, still laden with emergency aid, through the hectic commotion of central Fez but managed to toss Ingrid's phone across into my lap.

'What's this?' I asked, running my fingers over its screen.

'Ingrid left it in here when I had to take her to the hospital, look at that message from Aziz Bourkh,' Ayoub replied, looking over his shoulder and taking action to avoid a big old truck tearing off the front of the pick-up.

'Have you read the whole thing?' I asked.

'I don't know the password, do you?' he responded.

'No, I've no idea. You think Ingrid would do that. Tell Aziz that we are using the Merc to ship the contraband? That's good in some ways; you know why? Because we're not. Even if they intercept the Merc they won't get anything. The police can pull it over, the traffickers can too, none of them will find anything in that Merc. What they will get is Fiona, and her mood. She's so pissed off, she'll give them a right mouthful'

'I'd quite like to see that,' Ayoub said wryly.

Outside, the traffic was settling down. In the cab we weren't panicking, yet. The Hilux had long since passed the royal palace and was in a line of vehicles heading out towards the mountains.

'I don't understand why Ingrid would double cross us though, why would she do that Ayoub?

'Maybe she thinks she's got more to gain from getting in with Aziz, than she'll get out of us.' Ayoub replied, 'If you stop and consider our plan for a second or two, you could easily wonder whether it will actually work.'

I nodded in agreement, 'If Aziz can get his hands on the goods we've bought from the Rif without paying us for them, he'll make a massive profit. Some of that he could well have promised her. We don't know for certain though, but it would make sense of that message. Shame we can't read the whole conversation, that would be revealing.

'You know bro, I had a funny dream last night. I was peering through a window but it was blurry, like it was smeared with something. You couldn't see through it but there was a figure on the other side. I just couldn't make out who it was. They were female, I could tell that. At first I thought it must be Fiona, but maybe it was Ingrid. It felt like a warning though. I didn't get a good feeling from it.'

Ayoub sighed, 'You should contact Fiona, and give her a warning, or at least tell her to expect to be stopped at checkpoints,' I'd already begun to hear the ring tone on Fiona's phone when I heard Ayoub finish by saying, 'and tell her she should be cooperative.'

CHECKPOINT

'You like all the blue, Kasha?' Ayoub asked.

There were three of us in the hotel room. I was on the balcony overlooking the medina rooftops. Beneath me the town of Chefchaouen spilled down the hillside towards the river below, and behind the mighty limestone peaks of Tissimlane and Sfihna Telj towered over the scene. Hussain was making tea, and Ayoub was getting dressed. I'd read about the jewish emigration to this part of Morocco in the mid 1930's, how their persecution in Europe had driven many to find a new life in northern Africa, and that their painting of the medina walls in the colour of heaven had been an act of hope and aspiration.

'It's beautiful, Ayoub,' I replied, raising my voice above the sound of a dog barking somewhere in the twist of tiny streets below. 'The town's like a treasure, a jewel in these mountains.'

'Well the Jews certainly knew how to make business with the Berber farmers, my friend,' Hussain interjected.

I could hear him pouring tea, and just detect the sweet aroma of a Tuareg brew. It didn't surprise me that someone Ayoub knew had the hospitality skills and desert knowledge to rustle up such a tonic, but I hadn't expected to be drinking such a delicacy in the Rif mountains. Nor had I expected to see Ayoub changing into clean, business-like clothes. As I moved from the balcony back into the hotel room I gave him a quizzical look.

'You're best to make a good impression with these peasant farmers,' Ayoub said, 'you think the traffickers rock up looking scruffy and poor, nah they're badass! You'll be fine, they'll just

123

think you're a European with money, it's me that's got to look the part otherwise they'll start to ask questions and that makes things more complicated. They don't need to know anything about us. That's right Hussain, isn't it?'

I'd sat down at a wooden table nestled up against the wall by the door to the room, above which was a black and white photo of the king, Mohammed 6, looking cool with a cigarette in his hand. Hussain, sitting at the same table, offered me a small glass of the hot bedouin tea and agreed with Ayoub, 'Yeah, the farmers from Bab Berred know me, if you look like you fit in they won't worry. Anyway, when we meet them tonight they'll not be there for chatting. They'll just want to get their hands on the money, check it and go.'

Lifting his own glass of tea Hussain continued, 'Inshā'a Allāh, it'll be easy but we'll need a decoy once we've paid for the goods. Doing business at night time reduces the risk of things going wrong. Think about it. There's no risk of accidental witnesses for a start, and in the dark no-one can really get a good look at each other. It's easy for everyone to say they saw nothing. The decoy will mean we won't get ripped off. It'll just be like any other deal, ultimately everyone gets what they want. No-one will know who exactly was involved, or be able to inform the Macadam because it all happened well after evening prayers and sundown.'

*****

An hour out of Fez earlier the same day, on the well cultivated and agricultural plateau between the Atlas Mountains and the Rif, Ayoub and I had pulled into a town called Zaida. Here the Hilux had been emptied, except for the gypsum bags and our other accessories, at a Red Cross warehouse in the centre of the town. The staff there were suitably grateful, and gave us a short thank-you letter to present to the expats back in Ghazoua.

After Ayoub had done his dhuhr prayers, and I'd tried once again unsuccessfully to make contact with Fiona, we set off north out of the town towards the ragged Rif mountain escarpment. It wasn't long though before we joined a line of stationary vehicles waiting to pass through a police checkpoint. Built on a crossroads, Zaida is a strategic gateway from the south and west for any traffic going in or out of the Rif, and hence an ideal spot for the gendarmes to monitor and control the movement of people and goods.

Traffic was being stopped in both directions, and on the right-hand side of the road a coach had been pulled over, the contents of its luggage compartment lying in an untidy tangle beside an irrigation ditch. A white plastic cabin, probably incredibly hot inside, was positioned on the left side of the road giving the checkpoint an air of semi-permanence and authority. Progress across this checkpoint was slow, unlike in Mogador where most vehicles were waved through; it seemed like almost all the traffic was being scrutinised.

Ayoub could sense this, and said, 'If they ask us what we're doing we'll tell them about the aid we've dropped off with the Red Cross, and how we're driving up to Tetouan and then onto Tangier to give the Hilux back to the hire company. There's only one road through the Rif and to Tangier, so it makes sense.'

'Okay.' I acknowledged, 'I've got my passport and the Hilux's insurance stuff here, do you need your ID?'

Ayoub nodded, pulling a well thumbed identity card from the dashboard and adding it to papers on my lap.

Tension rose in the cab. I wound my door window down to get ready. All told there were six gendarmes at the checkpoint, all of whom were immaculately dressed, and armed with holstered handguns.

Eventually we were beckoned forward by a gendarme, his eyes concealed behind replica aviator Raybans and beside him his colleague was clutching a clipboard.

Leaning into the cab to get a good look at us both, the gendarme spoke as though we were his to command, 'Documents!'

I obliged him, passing all our papers into his outstretched hand, and we watched him retire to the cabin where no doubt he did some cross checking, or perhaps did nothing and just enjoyed delaying us.

When he returned a minute or two later with our documents he was all smiles. Bending, he handed them to me through the door window, and then said, 'Kasha?' as a question, rather than a statement.

I tensed up, the hair on my neck prickled, I tried to breathe normally and turned my gaze from the gendarme to Ayoub.

He took a long breath in, reached out with his hand to grasp the blanket that had been rolled up on the dash, lifted it slightly and said, "casha?'

The gendarme smiled again,

'It's nothing,' he said, and stood up to let us drive forward and away.

Once we were well and truly out of sight of the check point I cleared my throat and asked, 'Why do you think he said Kasha like that?'

'It's weird, isn't it.' Ayoub replied. 'You haven't managed to get through to Fiona either have you? We need to be really careful, it feels like something's going on.'

THE WELL

Water is a scarce resource in Morocco. More than two thirds of the kingdom's rural communities do not have clean, piped running water, with the result that these people rely on hand-dug wells that tap into naturally existing aquifers. Many households and communities in the countryside will have to travel some distance to access the groundwater from these wells, all of which are unlicensed and not tested for purity or contaminants. Hand-digging a well requires considerable skill and bravery. Locating the aquifer is carried out by a venerated local man or woman with a reputation for water divining, most often using a pendulum. Once a site has been established two men will begin chipping and digging at the ground, creating a hole approximately 1.5m in circumference. They will persevere, passing buckets of debris to a third man on the surface, through layers of silt, shale, limestone and sandstone until the vertical shaft reaches the depth of the water table. As a rule of thumb these hand dug wells are eight to ten metres deep, have two buckets on rope with a pulley, and will have cost about 1000 dirham a metre to dig.

*****

The bottle of spring water that Fiona had stopped to buy in Zaida was from a commercial well in the northern Atlas Mountains. Its label pictured a fertile hillside with terraced plantations, a winding and precipitous road, and a clear blue sky. Although it was from a different region, the label depicted a scene much the same as the one sweeping before Fiona now.

Leant against a hillside stone wall in the heart of the Rif mountain range, she sipped from the plastic bottle, eyeing the row of beehives that had led her to pull over and park.

Since leaving Fez at dawn, driving across the richly cultivated plain from the Atlas to the peaks of the Rif, she'd felt increasingly content. Happy to have left Kasha to his own nonsense. There'd been a slightly disarming moment at the police checkpoint outside Zaida when a delay with her documents had given her cause for what she thought was some entirely undeserved anxiety. However, the gendarme had apologised for the problem, an unusual occurrence in Fiona's experience, and she'd been able to push on into the amazing and mountainous landscape all morning.

Now, before lunch, she wanted to investigate the beehives on the slope slightly above where she'd parked. Setting off towards them she caught the attention of a nearby farmer, concealed and shading himself beneath a cedar tree. Busy cutting kiff, he took a moment to watch her, and then picked up his phone to make a call.

Fiona loved bees. She felt somehow akin to them; their queen, workers and male drones creating a social structure that seemed much better balanced and harmonious than any human equivalent. Clambering over the rocky ground to the hives, she could feel her spirits lifting, and she enjoyed sharing time around the hives with the farmer who'd popped up out of nowhere.

Once she'd returned to the Merc to continue her journey to Tetouan there was a lightness in Fiona's heart. She'd already passed over a couple of really high and exposed summits since leaving Zaida, and it was as she was proceeding up a series of zigzag cutbacks towards another summit, that she first noticed the black SUV in her side mirrors. There had been parts of the trip through the mountains where the road had been pretty busy, especially in the lower territories where there were more inhabited settlements, with farm machinery and livestock. Now though the traffic was thin, mostly made up of intercity coaches and lorries that whilst being cumbersome on the crumbly and narrow roads were relatively infrequent. The black SUV therefore stood out, and as it closed up behind the Merc's rear bumper a tension rose within her. Then, unmistakably, she heard the vehicle's horn go, and it pulled alongside the Merc.

The road ahead was empty. Looking left into the vehicle she could see three men. The one in the back seat being the farmer she'd met by the beehives, and the one in the passenger seat with a moustache was holding up what looked like a police badge and indicating that she should pull over. The SUV hooted its horn again, and so with a sigh she pulled over to the verge, parking up beside a deserted goat pen and well.

The beehive farmer stayed in the SUV, but the two well-dressed men from the front seats exited the SUV and sauntered up to the Merc. The road was completely quiet, and whilst Mr Moustache walked round the Merc, Fiona ran her driver's side window down to greet his colleague. He held up his fake 'nationale security' badge, removed his cap and spoke in French, 'Vos documents, s'il vous plait.'

This was a good start since Fiona was quite capable of speaking in French. She handed over her passport and documents, and waited while the two official-looking men scrutinised them. The man without the moustache then folded the vehicle documents and slipped them along with Fiona's passport into his back pocket. Looking at Fiona through the open door window he asked, 'Do you have any drugs or illegal substances in the car?'

'What!?' Fiona replied, 'you must be joking.'

'No, I am very serious, Madame,' he continued. 'Please could you step out of the vehicle so we can search it.'

Fiona was getting used to this kind of treatment from

Moroccan officials. She didn't want to, but opened the driver's door and got out. Meanwhile the official with the moustache had opened the rear door of the Merc and was beginning to rustle through Fiona's belongings. She noticed him, but before being able to object she felt his colleague touch her back, and spin her round so she was facing the car.

Provoked and angry, Fiona spun back around and hit the official across his face with her open hand, knocking his sunglasses to the ground. Mr Moustache, with his head in the back of the Merc, stopped still, and then shuffled backwards to get a better look at what was happening.

Fiona was glaring, wild-eyed and furious at the so-called official in front of her. He took a long deep breath in, a red hand print was beginning to show on his face, and then with the grace of a ballet dancer he flicked Fiona round, clasped both her hands together, slipped a cable tie over her wrists and tightened it. Having restrained her, he pushed his palm into her back, pressing her hard up against the side of the Merc, eliciting a growl from Fiona.

'Abdul, this is the right Mercedes isn't it?' Mr Moustache asked, feeling a touch alarmed by the speed with which events had degenerated.

'You know it is Mohamed,' Abdul replied, 'I watched you check the registration details, it's the white Mercedes that Aziz told us to find. The one mixed up in trafficking. It'll be stuffed full. Huh...and they send a woman to drive it.'

Spinning Fiona round again, Abdul met Fiona's snarling stare with his own. Holding her chin in his hand, he addressed her, 'You can try to treat us as fools if you like, but you're the one messing with forbidden things. Make it easy for yourself, tell us where the drugs are hidden and where you got them from. Maybe we can do a deal.'

Fiona was shaking with fury, 'There aren't any drugs you

pathetic man!' she cursed and then spat at him.

'We'll see,' he said, pulling her away from the Merc and ushering her towards the open stone pen and water well.

There was saliva on his hand where Fiona's spit had dribbled from her mouth, and he wiped it on her back as she stumbled over the uneven ground. His colleague with the moustache took her elbow in a semblance of assistance, helping her to turn and sit on the edge of the well, her hands still bound tightly.

'What were you doing stopping near where this man, this farmer, has his bees? Abdul asked, his face now ablaze with the red palm print. 'This is where you were collecting the drugs?'

Fiona stared straight ahead, and shook her head.

Turning to Mr Moustache, Fiona's inquisitor said, 'Take her foot and lift it, let's see if we can get her to speak the truth.'

As instructed, his colleague grabbed her left foot and raised it. Fiona's balance wobbled, she hadn't been prepared for this and instinctively reached back with her bound arms outstretched. Her centre of gravity cascaded backwards and her spine arched, sending her right foot kicking out into the air.

Someone shouted in alarm, but it wasn't Fiona. Speechless with terror, she saw blue sky, and then the concrete lip of the far side of the well as her head dropped backwards and she slipped into the shaft.

There was nothing beneath her. Dropping downwards into the black void she was swallowed by the damp empty darkness. Until, a hand tightened on her ankle, her body pivoted on the man's grasp, and she swung upside down, her body beating hard against the wet stone wall. There she dangled, a frenzy of fear in a dark abyss.

Above there were raised voices of panic, and the water bucket pulley rattled in mad disarray. Its rope, rough and flailing, brushed the skin on the back of Fiona's neck. She twisted, trying to catch it between her bound hands. Amidst this turmoil her sock was sliding down her ankle, the man's hand squeezed tighter but there was no grip. It slid from her foot with her shoe, and she fell headlong into the hole.

From above there were several muffled thuds as Fiona's body hit the side walls of the shaft on her way down. Tangled in the rope, she dragged the pulley clattering down behind her. She and it coming to rest in a final crash that petered out into an ominous silence. Mr Moustache still had her sock and shoe in his hand. He tossed them into the well. Rubbing his hands together, he thought about what he'd tell Aziz and whispered,

'Inshā'a Allāh.'

SCORING

'**M**erci pour votre compréhension' the sign had said as it was lit up by the Hilux's headlights. It was the third or fourth such message from the department of transport that had shone brightly back at us from the dark, snakey road that we'd been following into the mountains. Avoiding precipitous climbs the semi-tarmacked road had been built to hug the flowing river that wandered between the steep valleys of the region. Serving the scattered communities living along the road, it also provided access to the terraced farmland,. and cultivated cannabis plantations above through rutted dirt tracks. Although it was late, and we'd been driving for a while, we were wide awake, scanning the eerie landscape in front for our signal.

The three of us had set off from Chefchaouen at sundown, the Hilux loaded with our equipment and three large rolls of cash for our contraband stowed deeply in my shoulder bag. Ayoub had insisted that he and Hussain pray before our departure, giving me a little bit of privacy to try Fiona again. The call went unanswered so I left a voice message showing up as being sent, but not delivered.

'You get through?' Hussain had thoughtfully asked on returning from the mosque near our hotel.

'No, I left her a message. I think maybe she's having some alone time,' I replied, biting my top lip in unconscious reassurance.

'It could be a bad connection,' Hussain offered, 'the mountains and the poor network make it unreliable. I should not worry my friend. I'm sure she'll be in touch soon.'

Setting Fiona's fate or predicament aside hadn't been hard once I was driving and we were underway. The valley road required all my attention as it meandered in loops and cutbacks, at times crumbling at its edge into the river and on occasion only just being passable as we skirted rock falls. There was plenty of evidence of rebuilding and repair work being carried out following the earthquake. Several stone bridges were still in a state of semi repair, their improvised steel supports creaking and rattling as I picked my careful way across them.

Our contact signal had been incredibly faint at first, barely visible, but as we continued it became clearer and brighter, until as we made our way up an incline the light of a waving torch could clearly be seen. Nearing the light source a collection of white and worn stone buildings emerged from the darkness on the right hand side of the road. They themselves were dwarfed by the jagged outline of mountain peaks against the starry heavens above. One of the dwellings was a two storey home, with windows only on the second floor. Attached to it was a shop, displaying a tabac sign with three interconnected blue circles hanging above its door.

Our headlights revealed much of the quiet, night time scene, however it wasn't yet possible to fully discern our host holding the torch. It wasn't until we'd pulled up outside the shop that we could see there were two tall and thin djellaba-clad men, standing beside a large steel gate and its open entrance way. There were no smiles, simply a flash of the torch to indicate that we should pull through the open gateway and into the compound beyond.

*****

The back room of the hanoot was surprisingly big. The three of us had been accompanied by the two men from the road into the dimly lit space, where Hussain had led formalities and we'd been directed to a work bench on the far side of the room. Hussain had warned us not to ask questions, or seek to exchange names, our introductions serving merely as a way to start business, and being good muslim etiquette. Beside the bench a third man greeted us with an outstretched hand. He was younger than his associates, dressed in jeans, a tee shirt and a cord jacket, but his hands were already worn by a life in the fields. He was missing his two front teeth, and his grin made me want to look away.

Seeing my skin, he spoke in broken English until I hastily assured him that Arabic was fine. He then continued by pointing to the pile of 1kg slabs of contraband behind him, and the huge wooden pressing machine adjacent to the bench that was used to compress the pollen and create the slabs. He assured us that what we were buying was the finest, premiere quality, and to prove it he removed a lock knife from inside his coat and slit the cellophane wrap covering one of the slabs. Levering the package open the rich and intense aroma of the pollen wafted into the air around us. It was unmistakably strong and vibrant, just exactly what we had wanted, and what we'd promised Aziz Bourkh. By now the six of us were all standing by the bench, and Hussain once again took the lead suggesting that I show our hosts the money, and we begin business.

The older men and I sat on some low chairs near the door, with a small round table between us. They had grey, wiry beards, brown dull eyes and had pulled their djellabas up, revealing their sandals and hard worn bare feet. I put three large rolls of money on the table, and watched as one of the men leant forward, picked up one of them and scrutinised it. Giving his friend the other two rolls, he opened the first and began counting. His thin fingers, boney and bejewelled, setting out 1000 dirham piles on the table between us. Beside the bench Ayoub and Hussain were steadily checking each of the 60 slabs of merchandise, stacking them neatly in two bundles that were then taped together and packed into two of the blue gypsum sacks. Hussain had already removed his 1% commission to avoid any confusion. The sacks were then glued shut, carried outside and dropped into the back of the Hilux. It felt like the deal was going smoothly, just as Hussain had predicted.

The men opposite me eventually finished counting, and stood up as if ready to bring business to an end. They'd had a constant dialogue throughout the process, most of which I'd not understood. The younger man read the room, and began likewise to make himself ready. With matters apparently finished Hussian directed us back to the Hilux, where we said our farewells, and drove with our purchased contraband from the compound into the dark night.

*****

'We haven't got long,' Hussain said.

Our headlights lit up the narrow road, cutting a path into the gloomy landscape. From my open window I could smell the damp air and aroma from the plantations above, and if it hadn't been for the purr of the Hilux I could probably have heard the river.

'That went really smoothly,' Ayoub commented, seemingly ignoring Hussain's warning.

'Yeah, those farmers want to sell their product. They've got Eid next week, need money to celebrate, so it's a good time to buy. They want to make things easy,' Hussain replied. 'But we need to stop and get those sacks into the river, otherwise we're going to get caught and end up with nothing, or even worse.'

'You really think we need to do this, Hussain?' I asked.

'Yes! And the sooner the better,' he replied, 'pull over and stop where the road meets the river. It's about a five minute drive, you'll remember the spot. It's just before the road starts to climb up into the trees and around the side of the valley. The road there's been rebuilt with an overflow shoot into the river that we can use. Just keep going and I'll tell you when.'

*****

Ayoub was a semi-expert in assembling the truck tyre as a floatation device, having spent his childhood fishing and beachcombing in Mogador. Using the lights of the Hilux to see, he inflated one of the inner tubes, and then laid the net over the top of it leaving half of the netting spare and overhanging. He then laced the rope through the holes in the net and around the circumference of the tube. Standing on the netting to check it was secure, I could see him smiling at me.

'Do you think the water's going to be cold?' I asked.

'Yup, but you'll get used to it. I reckon it'll take you three hours to get down to Chaouen from here. It'll still be dark.....helpful.' He jumped off the tubing, collected the two blue sacks and laid them side by side on top of the netting. Looping the spare net back over the sacks, he tightened it all down, lacing the rope through the net again and around the tube. 'There you go,' he said with some satisfaction.

All in all it had only taken a quarter of an hour. He and Hussain launched me and the tubing into the river, which was too deep to stand up in. Hauling myself onto the tube, I watched their headlights flicker and then disappear into the tree line above. I was alone with the burble and wash of the flowing river, just the stars above and my thoughts for company. In the Hilux Ayoub and Hussain were planning the next stage of proceedings. It was important that some information was relayed to Mustaffa, and the pair were just agreeing a schedule, when the shadowy outline of a donkey and its cart blocking the road came into sight. Ayoub slowed the Merc and four figures emerged from the tree-lined verge to stand shielding their eyes from the headlights.

'Don't get out, let me do the talking brother. They'll want to be paid....if not they'll take the goods back,' Hussain said, poking his head from the passenger window and calling the men over to him. He greeted them, they spoke for a minute or two, and then there was a silent pause when nothing was said. The road was blocked, Ayoub turned the ignition off and waited.

Hussain addressed the men from his seat, 'You must have us mixed up with some other people. There's just the two of us, we have only a little piece. It's for personal use, we don't have money.'

The men, almost completely shrouded in their djellabas and woollen hats, were impassive. One of them left the group and hopped into the back of the pick-up to search the bed. Another opened the passenger side door, and ruffled through the contents of the cab, likewise without any success, except for finding Hussain's stash that he put beneath his djellaba. They could see there was nothing in the cab and neither was there a wad of money. A phone call was made by the farmers, they eyed Ayoub and Hussain suspiciously, but after references to the brotherhood and what seemed like a mismatch of information, the donkey and cart were removed from the road. Starting the Merc, Ayoub breathed a tired and relieved sigh. Now all he and Hussain had to do was catch me further downstream.

TALES FROM MOGADOR: KASHA AND THE KIFF

A PDF

Flowing water sings, and if you listen very carefully it will speak to you. Alison had told me this, and it was her voice that I thought I could hear whispering across the surface of the river. Gliding on the rush and gurgle of the fresh mountain water, I'd watched the Hilux's lights disappear and felt alone. Beneath me the river was still benefitting from the spring rainfall, running with force and grace down through the valley. Caught in its current, I was surrounded by darkness. The indistinct shapes of trees, rock falls, shrubby outcrops on the waterside, and the black outline of mountain ridges above, were a background to my solitude. Yet I felt I had company too. Alison was talking to me, but I didn't hear her properly or at least didn't concentrate on what she was saying until I heard her mention his name. 'Ishmael, Ishmael,' she breathed across the flow.

Immediately I thought of the young man I'd come to know at the printing shop in Barnook. His thin frame, accommodating nature and interestingly equipped premises had made an impression on me. The tiny, centrally located shop provided basic photographic and reproduction services, affording locals, used to a simple and rudimentary life, the luxury of printing facilities without having to travel too far from their farms. On most days there would be a queue of men, standing and fidgeting beside the simple wooden counter of his shop, waiting for a new identity card, driving licence or official paper to be reproduced. The machines in the shop were worn and frequently out of order. Those that worked were held together with glue and bent paper clips, and blessed with the words 'bis millah' before being used. Upstairs Ishmael had installed a rudimentary studio with a light diffuser and a white backdrop, making in-house professional portrait photography a reality for the small country town. I had probably been his first and only european customer, and on the several occasions I'd visited his shop my presence had produced lots of goodwill.

'Ishmael, Ishmael,' Alison murmured again, as the river narrowed and the current picked up its pace. I held the netting beneath me, my fingers through its holes, and across my mind flashed a memory of the pdf that he'd printed out for me. My diary entries. I'd used the wifi in his shop to email him the document, which he'd charged me almost nothing to print. At the time I had been consumed in pride at the sight of my words and thoughts being printed out on paper. I was so excited to show it off. It had never occurred to me that I should insist on him deleting the email along with the pdf. I had just walked from the small shop with a smile in my heart, leaving him with the contents of my diary to read at his leisure. Why hadn't I been more careful?

Beneath me the inflated tube settled down again, drifting smoothly and slowly rotating in the wash of the river water. I felt like I was sinking though. What was to stop Ishmael reading my diary, and then going to speak to the Macadam? Some of the language he wouldn't have been able to understand, but he'd definitely be able to recognise Aziz Bourkh's name.

My legs were wet and cold, I was tired and a sick feeling swept through me. The pdf could have been read by anyone, all Ishmael had to do was email it to them. If the Macadam didn't have the skills to read through my writing then there certainly would be others in authority who could. On that basis I could assume that my recent diary entries, containing reflective thoughts about the plan we were now realising in the Rif, was common knowledge amongst the security services.

That was, of course, if Ishmael had made the effort to

retrieve the pdf and mention it to the Macadam. This could not be guaranteed. I had seen the lackadaisical atmosphere in his shop, the slow, easy state with which he conducted his affairs. I could easily imagine him disregarding the attachment to my email, and never thinking of it again.

Anyway, he didn't know my name, all he had was my email address and my arabic nickname. It was only a set of diary entries anyway, full of all sorts of ideas along with the references to Otto, Asfi, Aziz Bourkh, Mustaffa and Ingrid. If I was in my right mind, which it was hard to be floating down a river in the middle of the night, I wouldn't have entertained any worries about the pdf. However, I couldn't help thinking that it would be foolish to disregard something that Alison had provoked in me.

There was nothing that could be done now though. I resolved not to tell Ayoub or Mustaffa about my faux pas. How awful it would be if I was to become responsible for their lives becoming worse. What if they, and I, were to be arrested and then punished. This was their chance to get ahead, to make a decent life for themselves. My lack of forethought and care might be the ruin of it.

There was nothing in those diary entries about moving the contraband down the coast by boat or our Tangier connections. Perhaps if we could get out of the mountains we'd be in the clear. I rested my mind and tried not to think anymore. Alison's voice had faded, the song of water on rocks filled my ears, and my eyes were heavy. In a while I'd wash up in Chaouen, be collected and get some sleep. The days to come would reveal whether my diary entries from the past would affect our futures.

TALES FROM MOGADOR: KASHA AND THE KIFF

TRUST IN ALLAH

I hadn't slept. The journey downstream to Chaouen had taken longer than Ayoub had anticipated and it was shortly after he and Hussain had picked me up that the first chorus of dawn prayers began to echo through the mountains. I was wet through and a little numb, but was able to sense the unease with which the pair greeted me, and could tell there was something they needed to share. It wasn't until we'd stowed the sacks in the pick-up, alongside our belongings from the hotel, and driven back up to the town for coffee, that they revealed the change in our circumstances. 'We're going to have to split up,' Hussain had begun, 'there's been a problem.'

I looked at Ayoub, who was dimly lit and sat on the cafe bench opposite me. We were outside but it was private. The street was empty, shop doors were closed. A man cycled past ignoring us, his sandalled feet pushing hard to peddle up the steep incline. Inside the cafe a radio was playing. 'It's Fiona,' Ayoub said, responding to my look, 'at least we think it might be her.'

'What do you mean, it's Fiona,' I responded, 'what's going on?'

Hussain, who was stirring his coffee, caught my gaze and said, 'All night there have been media reports of a road traffic accident on the mountain pass between Zaida and Tetouan. At first neither of us thought too much of it. But then the reports got more detailed and they mentioned a white Mercedes being parked on the side of the road.'

I swallowed and felt cold.

Ayoud scratched his chin, 'There's a Facebook post that says the accident involved an older white foreign woman, that she's been taken to Tetouen along with her vehicle, and that she's in a critical condition.'

I put my head in my hands and breathed out a long slow breath, 'That's why I couldn't get through to her, isn't it. Are there any details about what happened?' I asked.

'Not yet,' replied Hussain, 'what you can be sure of though is that there'll be tightened security all over this region now. The police road checks out of the mountains are going to be extra tough.' Staring directly at me he continued, 'You need to get to Tetouan as soon as possible, go to the police, explain that you were travelling with Fiona. That you were in Zaida dropping off the earthquake aid, and that you've just arrived and heard the news. This will help the authorities understand her broader story, and calm matters down a bit. The TV news is saying that the police are investigating the incident, but have ruled out terrorism and foul play.'

'Have they indeed?' I shot back, 'I wonder what on earth happened.'

*****

Hussain left for Tangier in a shared taxi an hour or so later. We'd all smoked several cigarettes, and put together a semblance of a plan. By travelling separately we hoped to avoid being associated with any rumours about three strangers spending big money in the Rif. I was to take my things and travel by bus to Tetouan. Ayoub had the most to fear for he had to drive the Hilux with the gypsum sacks full of contraband through the checkpoint outside Chaouen, and on to Tetouan. I was impressed by his attitude towards this undoubtedly perilous task. He said he would trust in Allah and had nothing to fear. Before parting we resolved to meet each other in Tetouan, partly to inspire hope but mainly so that final arrangements could be made with Mustaffa.

*****

The bus station, situated at the foot of the hillside upon which Chaoen is built, had been full of mid-morning business, and I'd taken my aisle seat in a state of semi-exhaustion and shock. In front of me a traditionally attired older man positioned himself in the aisle and began to address the bus's passengers. He was selling a menthol ointment whose properties he assured us were perfect for back and joint aches, and came in a fetching little square box with a camel on it. He was largely ignored by the other passengers on the bus, which I thought was a shame, so I asked him how much the ointment was. Later on I scolded myself for not paying 20dh and having a sweet present to take to Fiona's hospital bedside. After him a busy younger man drifted up and down the bus aisle touting a collection of electronic items. This man was completely ignored by the other passengers, and departed without a sale or even an enquiry.

Then, just as the bus felt like it was about to leave, a third and final visitor began an impassioned speech from the aisle. Unlike the two previous entrepreneurs, this man stole the complete attention of all those sat facing him on the bus. He had pathos, and although he spoke in complex arabic whose detail was lost on me, he had a hold on his audience. This became doubly apparent when he drew to a close, and a flurry of coins and notes began to be passed to him. He had obviously hit a vein of empathy amongst my fellow travellers, and after he and I had a brief conversation I too donated to his cause, whatever it was.

*****

Ayoub's cause was his own. He had made a commitment to

this plan and wasn't going to turn his back on the opportunity now. The stakes had always been high, with the possibility of a long prison sentence, or worse if he was caught. Now there was even more jeopardy with the news about Fiona. Alone in the Hilux he put his elbow on the open window ledge of his door, and reminded himself that he was travelling through a beautiful land. A land whose creation had been the will of the Almighty, and so too his fate was going to rest in the will of Allah.

Some 30km out of Chaouen, not too far from Tetouan, he eventually joined a queue of traffic waiting to get through the inevitable police checkpoint. Everyone was being stopped and questioned. This felt like a moment when he was about to learn whether his faith and devotion had any bearing on his mortal future.

Ahead he watched as two gendarmes led their alsatian dogs to the rear hatch-back of a dilapidated red peugeot. The taxi and lorry immediately in front of him waited whilst the dogs jumped into the peugeot and began their detection routine.

Another of the gendarmes dealt with the taxi quickly, knowing that the driver would never risk his livelihood by transporting anything forbidden, and as it pulled off he waved both the lorry and Ayoub through the checkpoint with a flick of his hand. Passing the gendarme Ayoub kept his eyes on the road.

'How fragile destiny is,' he thought to himself. Moments ago his future hung in the balance, the trained nose of a dog being the difference between rotting for years in prison or a chance to buy land and raise a family. As his heart rate began to slow, and the relief of getting through the checkpoint sunk in, he looked to the sky and muttered, 'Shkran.'

DAMAGED STOCK

From the stern railings where Mustaffa stood there was a fearsome drop down to sea level. He didn't suffer from vertigo under normal conditions. At sea though he'd felt sick watching the harbour pilot step from the hull door, 70 feet below, onto his small port authority craft. Its deck rose and then fell, on the peaks and troughs of the ocean beyond the harbour breakwater, precariously close to danger and death. The Mama Wats had sailed from the port at Tangier with all hands on deck an hour ago. Ahead of it lay a four day voyage through the Straits of Gibraltar and down the West African coast to Agadir. Behind the mighty 100m long cargo vessel stretched a tail of white wake water, its froth and noise the only turmoil on a calm ocean surface.

Mustaffa still had several hours of his daytime shift to go, and was busy checking the navigational lights and fixings on his maintenance schedule. His fixed term contract as an Able Seaman for the voyage had specific upkeep and sanitation duties, which were menial but important safety tasks, and ones he was familiar with from former fishing days. In addition he had been involved in the final battening down and securing of the freight, which had given him ample opportunity to locate the three gypsum sacks that Ayoub and he had dropped off earlier. They were now locked away in the cabin that he shared with a young Indonesian sailor working the night shift.

*****

'Do you think Mustaffa will be okay?' I asked.

Ayoub and I were sitting in the Hilux around the corner from the main police station in Tetouan. For many years the police had been based within the walls of the medina, but development, expansion and some increased prosperity had led to its relocation on the perimeter of the city. In front of us was Fiona's Merc.

'Yeah, he was nervous, but I think he'll be fine. I drove him into the docks, we stashed the gypsum sacks in a container for damaged stock, and then I left him to go through security.'

'Damaged stock?' I asked.

'Yeah, there's always a bit of freight that suffers in transit, mostly during loading. The skip with these bits and pieces in is still part of the inventory and gets loaded last. Mustaffa reckons he'll be able to remove the sacks from the skip on board later.'

'Let's hope so. I thought he was a bit withdrawn and quiet when you were going through how to set up the stuff. You know the inner tube, netting and rope. He's probably familiar with all that though, you think?' I added.

'He knows all about how to rig that stuff, he was a fisherman, Kasha! He was probably hung over. I just hope he doesn't get cold feet, drink a load of whiskey and miss his Hilal contact,' Ayoub responded.

'Or check the other sacks too thoroughly,' I said with a smile.

'No, we don't want that. Let's go somewhere, away from prying eyes and load the Merc ready for your journey back to Mogador. I'll then head over to Tangier, drop this pick-up off at the rental place and take the train down to Marrakech. Show me that note you got from the gendarmes.'

Shuffling on the seat, I pulled the creased official 'Ministry of Interior' form from my pocket and Ayoub began to examine it. After a moment or two, he drew his finger across the embossed royal crest at the top of the form, and grinned at me. 'This will get you through any check point between here and Mogador, no questions asked!'

'Yes, we really can't complain about how obliging the gendarmes have been. At first they were really suspicious, which isn't surprising. Anyway, I told them how we'd driven up to Ziada with the earthquake aid, and how Fiona had gone on to do some antique shopping. They seemed to accept that. Their attitude changed even more when they had a look through my phone at the messages I'd sent when we couldn't get hold of her.

'You've been to see her?' Ayoub asked.

'Yes, the police drove me to the hospital. In a way her being in a coma may have actually helped our cause. I think they were genuinely affected by the experience of going to the ward and seeing her all bandaged up.'

'Makes you wonder what happened up in those mountains, doesn't it,' Ayoub mused.

'Well they're saying that a farmer found her lying by the Merc. It had its bonnet open and the engine was still running. He'd been tending his bees when he'd heard Fiona scream, and had trekked about half a mile over to the car to find out what was going on. The farmer is not a suspect or anything, and was the one to call the police. They're working on the basis that she'd stopped to check something in the engine bay and got her hair caught in the timing chain. Her injuries are kind of what you might expect from that sort of accident. Sounds horrific doesn't it.'

'It's awful! I can't even begin to think about what that must have been like.'

'Gruesome,' I agreed. 'It's slightly odd though. Her ribs were broken and they've done an operation on her back. Don't know how that happens.'

'God's will bro, Inshā'a Allāh,' Ayoub replied.

'When we left the hospital the officer in charge told me that he'd been sent a message via the embassy from Fiona's daughter. The Merc needed to be driven down to Mogador. He gave me the keys, that form you just saw, and took my passport details.'

ALL AT SEA

Mustaffa's bunk was narrow. He'd slept a dreamless first night aboard the Mama Wats dozing comfortably to the engine hum and sway of the ship. Waking early he'd passed his cabin mate, who was finishing his night shift, in the corridor outside the galley and rec room. The pair had got as far as exchanging nods and smiles, but not had the time, or inclination perhaps, to share much more. They'd see little of each other even though they shared the tiny accommodation space, their work pattern designed so that they disturbed each other as little as possible. This was probably for the best given that Mustaffa wasn't going to be on board for long and definitely didn't want to leave any useful information about himself with his cabin buddy.

Having eaten, he started work. The cycle of maintenance and safety checks, which he was required to perform three times during his shift, started at the forecastle and worked its way back from the bow. The daytime schedule called for him to check all the lines and cargo straps on the foredeck, and those at the stern, and then to complete his cleaning duties on the lower decks and bridge, as well as overseeing the laundry. Just before sundown his last task would be to inspect and wash down the navigation lights on the masthead, stern and side of the vessel.

It wasn't hard work, but he needed to be careful, especially when he was on deck. There he concentrated and was alert; mindful of the heavy shackles, hooks and lashing rings that congested the foredeck, and vigilant to the sway and pitch of the ship. In some ways the job suited him, and in a different life it might have been a potential career. The routine and challenge was motivating, and although he had a daily briefing to attend, the relative independence of his role gave him frequent opportunities to savour the vast space of the ocean. Some twelve miles off the coast there was no land to see, with only the horizon, and occasionally another vessel, for company. Cleaning the bridge had given him a chance to covertly log into the ship's starlink router, thereby gaining access to GPS and Whatsapp which he needed if he was going to successfully communicate with Abdul Lalife.

He had also been able to familiarise himself with the pilot's door on the lowest deck. This was the door cut into the side of the hull, approximately ten feet from the surface of the sea, that yesterday he'd watched the harbour pilot use. It could be opened with the use of a hydraulic handwheel, and had an automatic sealing mechanism making it able to secure itself, and be watertight, should it be left open. Conveniently there was a small antichamber by the pilot's door, where tomorrow evening he would be able to inflate the inner tube and assemble the netting on it, with a modicum of privacy. His day shifts meant his absence wouldn't be noticed until the following morning, by which time he would be long gone and the ship's captain would eventually register him with the authorities as missing overboard. As the day passed Mustaffa's confidence grew. Abdul Latife was expecting to hear from him later in the evening, and with his shift drawing to a close Mustaffa settled down to enjoy a little social time in the galley, eating and playing cribbage.

It was pitch black outside when he clambered through the bulkhead door onto the deck overlooking the cargo hold and its crane. Lights from the gantry and bridge lit the foredeck. The weather had remained calm, the ship was steady and above his head there was a clear starry night sky. Mustaffa had enjoyed a couple of drinks with the crew who had been in the galley, making his feet a little unsteady and his gaze slightly out of focus. Standing against the railings on the port side he could hear the rush of water passing the hull 70 feet beneath him, the deep dark ocean breaking in a surge of white crests against the huge steel ship.

From somewhere, fairly near, he heard the unmistakable plop of a dolphin or porpoise playing in the ship's wake. It was almost impossible to see anything at sea level beyond a few feet from where Mustaffa stood. He heard it again though, and then saw the sparkly flash of a three foot wide tail flicking wake water into the air and disappearing into the depths. The tail had been much more refined and tapered than how he'd remembered dolphin's to be. It wasn't grey or deep blue either, but golden and its shape had a feminine grace to it.

The phone in his hand lit up with a message from Abdul Latife. Mustaffa turned his attention to communicating with his friend from Hilal, confirming the route the Mama Wats was taking, and some general timings for tomorrow's pickup. Abdul appeared to have his end of the operation under control, and so with the logistics of their rendezvous in place Mustaffa bid farewell to his friend and retired to bed.

That night the water spirit would come to him. She would slip under his door as a sea snake, slide silently across the floor and appear on his bed in her human form. There she would use a golden comb to brush her hair and speak to Mustaffa in his sleep. They would touch, her hair would fall across his naked body, he would feel her kiss. Before leaving she would make him agree to a pact.

In the morning Mustaffa woke without any recollection of her visit, nor any notion of the commitment he had made, or its potential consequences.

TALES FROM MOGADOR: KASHA AND THE KIFF

INGRID

Ayoub could have travelled with Kasha back to Mogador, but he had Ingrid on his mind. Even amidst all the danger, fear and threat of failure of the past couple of days, he'd had a warm feeling inside. The kind of affirming contentment that comes from the tender touch of another human. He had a sense that he was not alone anymore, although he didn't know what to make of Ingrid. She wasn't like the Moroccan village girls or those from the town for that matter. He hadn't needed to ask for her father's permission to speak with her, and only been able to do so with a chaperone. He hadn't had to wait patiently for her to remove her hijab, in the company of her mother and aunts, to see her hair. None of the social expectations that he'd grown up accustomed to had been required of him to enjoy Ingrid's company.

Together, during that drive to Marrakech, they'd shared their dreams and fears without concern for propriety, and become tender beneath the hot sun. Ayoub had been moved by the whole episode. Even setting aside the quicksand incident, he could not stop thinking about Ingrid. He wondered if it was the same for her.

He had the deepest respect for his faith and its traditions, and would always shy away from Haram but he also trusted in the will of Allah. Since leaving her in the hospital all those days ago he'd come to believe that fate had played its part. That the invisible hand of destiny had brought Ingrid across his path, blessed them with intimacy and provided him with the strength and courage to save her. The train journey to Marrakech, via Rabat, had given him lots of time to think about what might develop, and what the future might hold for them together. Hence it was with disappointment, and an ache in his heart, that he arrived at the university hospital to find that she'd been discharged.

He still had her phone and so all that was left to do was to travel back to Ghazoua and hope that he would find her at home. The bus journey eastward, back to Mogador late the same day, was a portrait of everything he disliked about his current circumstance: his seat was dirty and torn, the man sat next to him smelt of urine, it was stiflingly hot, slow and cramped. He didn't want to have to be a passenger on an old battered coach anymore, nor did he want to have to sleep on the sofa in his mother's home.

Unlike his older brother, who tolerated the family's poverty, and accepted that he and his wife would share the same bedroom as his mother, Ayoub wanted more. Driving the Hilux had reminded him of the pleasure of independence, a luxury that he hoped the business they'd conducted in the Rif was going to provide him. Watching the arid countryside drift by from his window seat, Ayoub day dreamed of buying some land, building a home and raising a family.

*****

Locating Ingrid's home had been relatively easy. The expat community in Ghazoua were all disconcertingly familiar with each other, and Ingrid's profession was strikingly memorable. Ayoub only had to ask a couple of senior-looking foreigners at the Carrefour supermarket to get directions, and with a quickening to his heart he'd found himself knocking on the door of her home.

'Ayoub,' she said, practically singing his name. 'What a lovely surprise, come in.'

The long embrace Ingrid gave Ayoub set him at ease. She was dressed in a european-style summer dress with leggings. He thought she looked well and told her.

Smiling, she thanked him for her phone and beckoned him to follow her through to the kitchen where she began to prepare some tea.

'Have you eaten?' she asked.

'No, I've been a bit preoccupied,' Ayoub responded, taking a seat at the wooden table in the centre of the room.

'Me too,' she chipped in, lifting the lid of a tagine dish and scooping several ladles of meat and vegetables onto a plate. Putting it down in front of him, with a fork that he wouldn't use, she sat down opposite him and spoke.

'Did you look at the messages?'

'Couldn't help notice the one from Aziz,' Ayoud responded, as he inspected the tagine.

'Guess I need to explain?'

Ayoub looked Ingrid in the eye, 'That would help,' he said.

'Okay, so I went to Aziz about your plans to go to the Rif. Bad eh!'

'Not the best,' Ayoub agreed.

'You probably think I'm selfish. I was only trying to look out for my brother,' Ingrid continued.

'No, I might have done the same.'

'I needed money, Ayoub. I needed a ton of it and Otto had come up with this plan that I thought just might work. Everything was going fine but then something changed, Otto unsettled me.

'Yup, I've had the same feeling about Otto. I know what you mean.'

'That's good, at least we're on the same page about him!' Ingrid said, reaching out to touch Ayoub's arm.

'When he got back from Asfi he was all weird, I was desperate. I needed money to help Merek, and thought that if I did a deal with Aziz Bourkh then it would be guaranteed.'

'Aziz Bourkh,' Ayoub repeated.

'Otto seemed out of his depth, and I didn't know how reliable you or Kasha would be.' Ingrid was looking directly into Ayoub's eyes, 'What happened in the desert though, that showed me I should've trusted you.'

Ayoub was a bit lost in her blue eyes, but managed to reply, 'I should be angry......I know I should be.' Then reaching out to touch her arm, he whispered, '...but I'm not.'

'I'm so glad you're here.' Ingrid said, brushing her fingertips across Ayoub's brow. 'What happened in the desert, I owe you my life, I will never forget.'

Looking into her blue eyes, he said, 'This is our bond.'

Ayoub reluctantly broke the spell and beckoned her to sit beside him. 'Now you need to tell me everything so Kasha and I can make a plan.'

'So as well as Aziz, there's Otto to deal with! He read about Fiona's accident, it was all over social media and on the TV too. It rattled him so much that he couldn't sleep or eat. He started to look ill. Every time there was a knock on his door he thought some disaster or threat was about to befall him. He's such a little self-centred German man! He kept on calling here. I told him to just be calm and keep his head down. That didn't make any difference though. In the end he went to the police, I think, to protect himself. Goodness knows what they thought of him, probably not very much, but you have to assume that both Aziz and the police know everything. They'll be waiting at the beach for Mustaffa and the drop, and when you and Kasha show your faces in Mogador there'll be trouble.'

Ayoub stood up; he needed to smoke a cigarette.

ALL IS NOT LOST

Mustaffa had never been taught to swim. In a country where three quarters of the population cannot read or write a short simple statement, learning to swim is not seen as a priority. It is nevertheless an obviously important skill if you are working at sea. In the absence of formal lessons most fishermen pick up their swimming skills through trial and error, practising in the shallows in their youth until they gain their confidence. Many however never become strong swimmers, and so while they can remain buoyant they are limited and extremely vulnerable if they find themselves adrift in the open ocean. Mustaffa was well aware of his limitations, and so had sought out a life jacket earlier in the day. It now lay beside the gypsum sacks, netting, rope and semi-inflated tyre on the floor of the anteroom by the door in the hull used by the harbour pilot.

It had long since become dark. His second full day on the Mama Wats had passed by smoothly, and at one point he'd even imagined that with a different throw of fate's dice perhaps he might have returned to a seafaring life. For now though he had plenty of other things to occupy him, not least the immediate challenge of getting from the Mama Wats onto Abdul Latife's boat with the contraband, and then making it through the surf onto the beach by Moulay.

He'd managed to make contact with Abdul early in the evening before sun down. Together they'd triangulated a rough time and position where their respective paths might cross, and agreed a schedule of contacts to confirm progress towards that point. After sun down he'd heard from Abdul again, and this triggered Mustaffa to pack his few belongings and begin preparations to leave.

The inner tube did not take long to inflate, and any noise from the process was muffled by the low rumble of the ship's engines, and its creaking hull. He was tense, this was a very dangerous enterprise he was about to embark upon, he might easily slip through the water to his death at the bottom of the ocean.

The unexpected company of the ship's cat while he fastened the net to the tube went some way to distract him, as did the knots he'd tied. He had always loved the shapes and symmetry of knots, the way the lines would radiate out from the crossing point at the centre, like the art in the mosques or in the Quran. The simple purity of the shapes, whose pattern seemed to come from nowhere and yet have such strength.

Mustaffa stood back to admire his work. The ropes were lashed down, the sacks were in place, everything was ready. All that was left for him to do was to take to the main deck, and wait to spot the fishing lights on Abdul's boat to appear.

The captain on the bridge would probably be able to see Abdul's two and half metre carvel boat on his radar, but this would be of little consequence given that it was not unusual for ambitious fishermen to be working the shipping lanes. He would assume the fisherman would take avoiding action should it be required, and unlike inshore, where a night mist would be hanging over the water, the deep ocean where they were was clear, calm and moon lit. Navigation would be easy.

Mustaffa waited, his eyes searching the darkness across the water, and its rolling peaks and troughs. Time passed. He rubbed his eyes. Then, a long way off to the east there was a twinkle of light. It flashed and then disappeared. He stretched on his tiptoes and again caught sight of the shining light. 'That was it,' he thought, and dialled Abdul's number.

Moments later, having spoken to his friend, he was descending the stairs and sealing his phone in a waterproof bag.

This was it!

He stood in front of the pilot's door, spun the circular handle anticlockwise and with a heave pulled it inwards. The cool air and sea smell from outside poured in around him.

Turning, he lifted the inflated tube onto its side and rolled it to the open door space. There, standing 10 feet above the ocean's surface, he scanned the horizon hoping to see Abdul's lights again before he plunged into the ocean. He didn't see them, and paused.

All his fears returned at that moment. Might he just sink to the ocean floor?

Picking up the life jacket he slipped it over his head, whispered 'Bis Milah.' and jumped.

The tube fell into the darkness before him.

He heard it hit the water just before he felt the freezing grip of the ocean ripple up through his body, and cover his head.

The tube had landed on the far side of the wake wave pushing it away from the hull of the ship, Mustaffa however had been swept down the other side of the wave and in towards the ship.

The water engulfed him, cold and deadly, and when he rose through the buoyancy of his jacket the enormity of the ship towered above him.

Another wake wave swept him in towards the shadow of the hull, pulling him down its side and back towards the propellers.

He couldn't breath, his knuckles smashed against the unforgiving wall of steel above him.

Might he die a lonely death beneath this ship, or be cut to

pieces in the merciless blades that were sucking him in?

Frantically he clawed at the water, but it was hopeless, there was nothing he could do. The ocean was going to devour him, if the ship didn't crush or pulverise him first.

No one would ever know and perhaps no-one except his mother would ever care.

The end was all unravelling quickly, or was it slowly?

Was he above water or below?

Were these the last moments of his life, he couldn't tell.

He felt a warmth at the foot of his spine. A hand was hauling him back and upwards. It turned him, he felt soft lips upon his own and heard his name. His head broke the surface, he gasped for air, and at that moment saw the flash of a golden tail in the moonlight.

Bobbing on the rise and fall of the ocean he could see the Mama Wats pushing on through the water away from him, its night lights shining, and its tail of fluorescence marking the dark water behind it. For what seemed like a long time Mustaffa felt completely alone and abandoned. He was cold, had lost his cargo and from the surface of the water had almost no chance of seeing Abdul's small vessel.

It wasn't his destiny to perish there alone though. For out of the inky blackness came the chugging rhythmic beat of a small diesel engine, and the familiar sound of his name again. Not in the soft feminine tones that he'd heard before, when it was whispered in his ear. This time it was part of a panicked and searching cry, which was replaced with joyful shouts when the deck light from Abdul's boat picked Mustaffa out from the gloom. Initially blinded by the beam of light Mustaffa raised his arm to shield his eyes, and caught sight of the tyre tube and sacks tethered to the side of the blue fishing boat.

All was not lost.

SOUAD

'The police know,' was the first thing Ayoub had said when I answered his call.

I'd been eating lubea. The spicy bean dish, served absolutely everywhere in Morocco, was piping hot and served on a pretty china plate with an accompanying bread roll and melka. The Merc was parked up on the other side of the narrow city street, its keys lying on the table in front of me.

'Where are you?' Ayoub continued.

'I'm in Asfi,' I answered, 'just stopped to get some food. What do you mean the police know?'

I had a fairly decent idea what he meant, but was hoping that the pit of terror that had just opened up in my stomach was an overreaction.

'Otto's gone to them and told them everything. He read about Fiona online, got frightened and turned himself in.'

'Fuck,' I responded, 'how do you know?'

'Ingrid told me this afternoon when I got to her place in Ghazoua,' Ayoub answered. He was sitting on her doorstep, her cats mingling at his feet, the smell of her scent still lingering on him. 'I'm surprised that you didn't get pulled over on the way down from Tangier, I guess the police haven't coordinated a plan yet, but it won't be long. You know it feels like they've been onto us for a while.

'Anyway, you'll have to leave the Merc and go into hiding. We'll both have to, brother. Not only are the police onto us, but

Ingrid's told Aziz the whole of our plan including how Mustaffa's going to bring the contraband ashore, so we've got both the police and his gang on the lookout for us.'

I had stopped eating. Those around me continued with their meals oblivious to the calamitous news I was receiving. 'What are we going to do?' I eventually said.

'Get the sacks from the Merc, buy a hold-all and go to the medina. I'll drive up to Asfi on my bike, and pick you and the sacks up from Bab Chaaba.'

'Okay,' I agreed, trying to compose myself.

'It'll take me a bit over an hour to get to you,' Ayoub continued, 'it'll be good to travel at night time, they'll not be looking for either of us on a motorbike.'

'Where are we going to hide?' I asked.

'I'm going to hold up with Ingrid, reckon I'll be safe there. You'll have to work something out, bro. Let's talk when I get to Asfi.'

'Inshallah,' I replied, picking up the keys to the Merc and running my thumb over the one dirham coin that was still attached to the fob.

*****

Souad was waiting by the municipal well in Ain Lajar when Ayoub and I finally arrived. It was deep into the night, the air was cold and the sound of the diesel pump and splashing water covered the noise of our arrival. She hadn't been surprised when I had called her earlier, indeed it was almost as if she'd been expecting me to make contact. I had told her briefly that I needed some help, and without any hesitation or questioning she'd invited me to stay at her and her mother's home.

We followed the Fiat Uno, driven by her mother's

boyfriend, out of the village and up into the surrounding hills. There the road wandered through dry farmland and past isolated homesteads, all shrouded in the darkness and secrecy of night time. Somebody might hear our vehicles, but they wouldn't be able to see or identify us, and so when we finally arrived at Souad's secluded home, it felt secure.

The children were asleep. Souad fixed us tea, heated some bread and we sat by the open fire. Warmed by its flames, the day, our predicament and my exhaustion began to catch up with me. With sleepy eyes I listened to Souad tell us about the local gossip. It didn't fill me with confidence that people in the area were aware that something had alerted the police. She mentioned how the atmosphere at the checkpoints on the coastal road had become much more severe in the last day or two, and that there were lots of different stories about why the authorities were having a clamp down.

'They're after us,' I'd said to her, but she shook her head.

'If the gendarmes had really wanted to capture you two, you'd already be in jail. They're after someone else, someone with more power and influence than you two. The gossip is that they want to shake things up in Mogador, the controlling families have got too strong. The Macadam here in our village says that the authorities have been waiting for a chance to undermine the Jbala network. You two, mon cherie, are small fry in comparison.'

Ayoub and I looked at each other. Addressing Ayoub I spoke in English, 'So they're going to stake out the beach and think they'll catch Aziz red-handed smuggling drugs. Mustaffa's going to get a bit of a shock, isn't he.'

'Everyone's going to get a shock,' Ayoub replied, 'especially when they look in the sacks.'

ONCE BITTEN

She could feel the warmth of the sand on her belly. It was night time and he had his back to her as she approached, the murmur of the men's voices and their digging a background distraction to her slinking into the clearing. Winding herself up his trouser leg, without disturbing the tension in the material, she knew he wouldn't feel her presence until it was too late.

Then suddenly, he shouted and moved forwards. Instantly she bound her body tight around his leg, arched her head back and with all her might sank her fangs through his trouser leg and into the soft flesh inside his thigh. He shouted and then screamed, beating a hand down upon her.

Torch lights flashed across the ground as the other men reacted to commotion. She tightened her grip, and pumped her venom into his flowing blood.

There was noise everywhere now. The man stumbled, his heart racing. Blood oozed from around her mouth as he fell to the ground with his hands clasped to her head trying to pull her free. Far away the dogs were barking.

Cries of terror pulsated between the other men amidst the turmoil. In the blackness, clouds of sand were kicked into the air as panic and pain engulfed him. He twisted and writhed as the last of the poison entered him.

She let go, knowing her work was done. Soon the numbness would creep through each of his limbs, dulling and cramping his senses, until nothing was left and his spirit was driven from his body.

*****

It had been a surprise for Mustaffa to see two gendarmes on board the boat once Adbul had hauled him on board. He had not expected to see anyone else but his friend, especially so far out to sea, however he'd learned from an early age that there's no such thing as a secret in Morocco. The gendarmes were armed and dressed in waterproofs. They said very little, using their torches to direct him to sit in silence while Adbul turned the boat and set a course for the shore.

Over the next hour and half the fishing boat made steady progress across the calm ocean towards the mainland. Abdul and Mustaffa remained quiet, occasionally glancing with resignation at each other. One of the gendarmes had used his phone earlier, presumably to contact his colleagues, and did so again when the lights of Mogador crept over the ocean's horizon.

Having finished the call, the two gendarmes lifted the inflated tube and sacks over the side of the boat, and instructed Mustaffa to clamber aboard the improvised craft. He was to ride the incoming tide to the shore, bury the sacks as had originally been planned and then wait for the town police who would track him. Mustaffa couldn't believe his luck as the current swept him in towards the dark land. Perhaps there was a way he could escape once he landed.

*****

Aziz, and his gang of seven henchmen with their dogs, parked at the radar station on the beach. Two of the men disappeared into the building with bottles of wine and instructions for the operatives, and then the group began to trek up the shoreline. They had searchlights, but decided not to use them so as not to warn anyone of their presence. The dogs were let off their leads and circulated around the gang, periodically running off into the dunes and returning to paddle in the shallow incoming tide.

The sand underfoot was soft and not easy going. Aziz was hoping that they wouldn't have much further to go, scanning the darkness over the ocean as his steps grew tired.

Rounding a small headland on the beach the gang all stopped in their tracks, for there amongst the dunes to their right was the figure of a man. It was Mustaffa. His outline was only just distinguishable in the gloom, but unmistakably he was moving sand. The dogs were held by their collars and Aziz gave the order to wait. He reasoned it was better to just steal the treasure that this man was burying, than have to deal with him and then his dead body. So they waited.

Eventually Mustaffa finished, checked around him and then disappeared into the dark night. Aziz directed his men towards the clearing in the dunes where Musaffa had been. There, between clumps of beach grass, he stood with a searchlight in hand and watched while his gang dug.

They gathered, and pushed at the fine sand until the two gypsum sacks that Mustaffa had left began to emerge from the hole. In the background there was just the sound of the ocean on the beach, the occasional squawk from the gulls and their own voices. The dogs were sitting together unleashed on the far side of the hole, when their ears pricked up with interest. None of the men noticed. The dogs stood and then, with a flick of sand from their feet, disappeared into the blackness that surrounded the clearing.

Aziz just caught a glimpse of them leaving, but turned his attention to the sacks that were now free and lying beside the hole. Throwing a flick knife to the ground he indicated that the sacks should be opened, and that was when he first felt a weight on his leg. Ignoring the sensation, he shone the light directly at the sack, his expectations gathering as the knife was drawn through the tough plastic. It split and opened to reveal slabs of mud and straw tied together with string.

Aziz shouted in anger, and then felt her bite.

*****

Ayoub and I travelled to El-Sheba with Souad in the morning, and ate breakfast as she opened up her cafe. At our feet was a large hold-all. On the opposite side of the road a blacksmith was changing the wheel on a pony buggy. 'We are going to have to find someone else to buy our stuff,' I said to Ayoub.

'Yup, let's catch up with Mustaffa, and see if he's got any ideas,' Ayoub replied, smiling.

For the next exciting installment of Kasha, Ayoub and Mustaffa's adventures see 'Soloman's Seal', due to be published in July 2025.

ACKNOWLEDGEMENTS

Thank you to all those that helped and encouraged me throughout the writing of this book.

Special thanks go to:
My dear friend Luisa Schlotterbeck without whose support I may never have started in the first place.
My thoughtful and considered editor Pete McCarthy.
My daughters Perdie and Hannah, for all their love and care.
My sister, whose energy and enthusiasm for this first book provided important momentum in its closing stages.
And most importantly the Kingdom and people of Morocco, whose wonderful country has been my home for the past year.

ABOUT THE AUTHOR

Kasha Kermould

Kasha Kermould is a pseudonym for Angus Dawson.

Angus grew up in Scotland, graduated from Stirling University with a degree in Philosophy and Economics, and worked for 30 years as a teacher and senior leader in the state education system in England, UK.

For the next exciting installment of Kasha, Ayoub and Mustaffa's adventures see 'Soloman's Seal', due to be published in July 2025.

Made in the USA
Monee, IL
22 July 2025

21249486R00105